What are you looking at Bitch?

2nd Edition

MOHSEN EL-GUINDY

What Are You Looking At Bitch?
2nd Edition

ISBN:
Paperback 978-1-954341-38-8

The views expressed in this book are solely those of the author and do not necessarily reflect the views of the publisher, and the publisher hereby disclaims any responsibility for them.

Writers' Branding
1800-608-6550
www.writersbranding.com
orders@writersbranding.com

CONTENTS

CHAPTER I

Hashem El-Abbadi, a 35 years old engineer, descends from a prominent wealthy family in the United Arab Emirates. His family business in steel and aluminium industry emerged as the largest industrial conglomerate in the region.

After graduation from Princeton University, Hashem worked in his family business for five years, and then decided to go his own way and starts his own business. He founded a holding company engaged in conglomerate businesses across the world. The holding company owned many subsidiaries dealing with energy, oil and gas, petrochemicals, textiles, natural resources, retail, telecommunications, and high tech

Based on annual revenues exceeding 10 billion dollars, the holding company was considered among the top 50 conglomerates dealing with diversified businesses.

In addition to his several business commitments and obligations, Hashem fell in love with bodybuilding. He took the bodybuilding sport by storm. Four times a week he performs six main exercises that target the main muscle groups in his body. In order to be tanned, he would run over to the sea, jump in the waves, get the salt water all over, and get tanned all over his body.

Hashem was very good looking in a specific manly way. he was tall with a muscular body of a bodybuilder. Muscles ripple across every part of his body as if he were moulded from granite. His jet-black hair was thick and lustrous. His eyes were a mesmerising deep black. His face was strong and defined with sharp jaw and angular cheekbones. He moves with a lithe grace. Like all men who look this good, he had no interest in women. Women throw themselves at him, but he was not attracted to any of them as if none of them were beautiful enough for him.

As an extremely wealthy man, Hashem lives the life of the rich and famous. He roams the world visiting his subsidiary companies and also the most beautiful places. He drives the best sport cars, lives in luxurious houses, wears fine elegant clothes, and dines in fancy restaurants.

Angela Collins is a 30 years-old American and is sexually attractive. She had a pretty face framed by cascading brown hair. Her body was juvenile with full breasts, full lips, high cheekbones, small waist, and a round firm butt. She graduated from Pomona College in California and had a degree in business administration from Harvard business school.

When Angela's father died, she, as his only child, inherited a huge company in Florida producing industrial chemicals. After five years from running the company, she oversaw its expansion from 150 employees and $200 million in annual revenue to more than 500 employees and $500 million in annual revenue.

Angela Brown was regarded as one of the richest women in America; and rich men had sought her hand, but she rejected them all without even thinking.

Angela was spoiled in a very strange way as a child, because everybody told her, from the moment, she was able to hear, that she was marvellous. She never heard a discouraging word during her childhood. She grew up expecting people around her to do whatever she wanted. She became very good ordering everyone around. She was the princess; the house servants and maids were terrified of her.

Her father was a man with a temper, and people feared him. He gave Angela everything under the sun. While she was at school, every six months she had a new car, a Jaguar, a Mercedes, and she had $100 in her pocket every day. He raised her in many ways like a son. He wanted to control everything she did. He told her not to trust anyone, not to talk on the phone, he was domineering, he was a bully, but in Angela's eyes, he was a real man.

Angela inherited her father's tough, aggressive nature and his need to control. She was grateful to her father for making her a tough daughter. It helps her deal with dire situations.

When she grew into a beautiful young woman, the spoiled upbringing induced a sort of narcissism in her character. She admired her own attributes and believed that the world revolves around her. She lacked the ability to empathize with others, and she had this ardent desire to focus on herself all the times. She became arrogant, self-centred, manipulative, demanding, and aggressive.

When Angela gets nervous or angry, her right-hand shakes involuntarily. The doctor prescribed for her propranolol as a treatment. Pills of propranolol were always ready in her handbag in case hand shaking occurs.

The doctor also advised her that she must do some exercises in order to increase her energy level, and lower stress levels, and improve her overall health. He recommended 30 minutes of physical activity per day, five days per week.

Angela was fond of music, so she chose dance therapy as a sport. It is a type of therapy that uses movement to help individuals achieve physical and mental health. It also helps in reducing stress, anxiety and depression. Angela joined a dance club and with the help of an experienced instructor, she became a skilful dancer. Dancing provided her an excellent aerobic workout. Moving with music felt good and hilarious. Dancing became her passion.

Angela has never been on a date because she was not interested in men. The excuse she introduced to her intimate friends was that men seem to think that women exist solely for their pleasure and enjoyment, but in reality, women are full, complex beings, whose lives are much greater than what men think of them. The fact Angela was trying to hide however, was that she was asexual and lacked sexual inclination toward men. She has never been sexually aroused. She never gets horny. Her lack of arousal was because in her unconscious was the notion that all men are potential predators. Having sex with men is like raping or beating her. Angela feels unsafe in men presence She cannot stand them touching her.

All her life she had been told by her father that men are pigs. He told her repeatedly that if a boy is being nice to her he is trying to get in her pants. He told her to stay away from men and that they only do things for sex. What he taught her about men stuck with her until this day. She knew that he was trying to protect her, but what he did terrified her and made her afraid of men.

CHAPTER 2

In 2008 the world economy faced its most dangerous crisis since the Great Depression of the 1930s. The contagion, which began in 2007 when sky-high home prices in the United States finally turned decisively downward, spread quickly, first to the entire U.S. financial sector and then to financial markets overseas.

Just before the financial crisis occurred, Angela borrowed money from the bank to make her company afloat but to no avail. The company was going down. Her business was running out of money and bills were piling up.

In the middle of the financial crisis, it was difficult for her to diagnose exactly the shortcomings of her failing company. Two reasons however, were evident; poor budgeting and an abundance of debts and financial obligations.

Angela became plagued by anxiety, feeling of uncertainty, and worries about her personal effectiveness at work. Her anxiety was intensified after the collapse of the company. And although she got some relief from antidepressants, the drugs would falter every so often, plunging her into a deep, dark mood.

It was hard to get up and go to work. In fact, there were times when she simply couldn't drag herself into the office and called in sick. Her hand shaking increased and she started taking overdose from propranolol. She felt ashamed because she looked so exhausted and tired.

Angela had to put her company up for sale. She knew that selling her business is not a process she can turn over to her broker or lawyer. She will be the main player throughout the process. She should be prepared to answer probing questions and furnish specific documentation.

Angela loved her employees. She does not see them as a disposal part. She wanted them to work for her forever. She would feel awful if they leave her and work for other companies. Hundreds of workers are now threatened by the collapse of her company. During the selling process, she would do her best with the new owner to preserve her workers' rights.

Among the business activities of Hashem Abbas was to buy failing companies. In his view, there are good reasons to buy a failing business. A failing business may be unable to adjust to a new market or take on the challenge of Internet marketing. Before he decides on buying an existing business, he considers why the business is failing. For example: is the product or service the business offers obsolete or lacking customer interest? Is the business in a location that isn't prudent for what products or services it offers? Is the building in need of improvements; in other words, does it look closed down? How does the business do in the customer service area? Do customers complain or avoid the business? Is the business owner in debt to vendors or lenders and needing so much money that the only choice is bankruptcy? Do people even know the business exists? Is the business owner ready for retirement but has no heirs to run the business?

All of these are good questions to analyse and find answers to before Hashem makes an offer on an existing business. He has business management skills others do not have. He can turn business failure into success.

In his office, Hashem was having a meeting with the chief executive officer (CEO) of one of his subsidiary companies - The petrochemical company.

Hashem: "It has been always my opinion to have a strategic partnership between our petrochemical company and another company working in a related field to achieve a strategic goal."

CEO: "What makes you think of merging our company with another?"

Hashem: "Cost savings and revenue enhancing. Two companies together are more valuable than two separate companies are."

CEO: "Our company is doing fine. What are the benefits of merging then?

Hashem: Increasing sales, maximizing profits or increasing market share. There are other benefits like acquiring new technology, reaching new markets and grow revenues and earnings. I am thinking of product - extension merger - Two companies selling different but related products in the same market."

CEO: "So you are interested in diversification. Will it be a merger between national entities or cross-border merger?"

Hashem: "Cross-border merger would be more profitable for us."

CEO: "Do you have a specific company in mind?"

Hashem: I made some search and I found an American company dealing with industrial chemicals. The owner's name is Angelina Brown."

CEO: "We are not going to buy her out, are we?"

Hashem: "Buying her out is a big possibility, but for now I am thinking of a merger activity. The purpose is to improve margins, and increase market share. We will be just partners with us having the upper hand. Let us go there and talk to her in a friendly manner. Tell my lawyer to come with us to attend our meeting with the owner."

Angela's secretary received an e-mail from Hashem's holding company expressing his interest in negotiating a merger with Angela's industrial chemicals company. He would be visiting some of his subsidiaries in America from June 5th to June 8th, after which he would be available for only 24 hours. He asked for an interview with Angela on the 9th of June.

Angela said to her secretary, "Okay, send them my approval. Let's see what they have to offer."

In Florida, Hashem and his CEO and Lawyer sat with Angelina in her office discussing the merge. Angela's CEO and lawyer were also present.

Hashem: I am here to close a deal or walk away from it. If I am going to close the deal, I must be sure that it is positive for both sides. I want to negotiate with you a mutual beneficial deal.

Angela: "From my side the good deal must fall comfortably within the goals and limits that I have set for this particular negotiation? A good deal is one that is fair for both sides. The negotiation must end in win-win situation."

Hashem: To be sure that you have a good deal and a win-win situation, I have important questions to ask.

Angela: "Our position in the American market is strong. We have the upper hand."

Hashem: "You don't have the upper hand. We made thorough investigations and we know a lot about your company. Your company has experienced some sort of material changes, such as decline in profits, loss of major customers and loss of key executives."

Angela: "We have prepared for you all the documents we can offer."

Hashem:" I will look at these documents later. But now I need transparent answers. I want you to provide me with the quality of your inventory: overstocked or obsolete; the condition and amount of your receivables; what is the amount and status of your payables? Is there an order backlog? Do your good customer relationships justify goodwill pricing? Are all your licenses and government approvals in place? Copies of last three year's tax returns. I want to have accounting for past years in place."

Angela: "Negotiating isn't about taking advantage of other people. Deals only get done if buyer and seller find a mutually agreeable deal. Dead deals have been revived because of a willingness of both sides to continue talks toward a creative, mutually beneficial deal."

Hashem: "It's time to put some thought into how much your business is worth. Be realistic in pricing. You set a high price on your business before analysing its value. What you have to do before pricing is to assemble formal financial records for your business for this year and the previous three years."

"Be clearer please." Angela said impatiently.

Hashem: How long a business remains on the market is determined by its pricing. It is much better to complete a valuation process, which can then be used to justify the price. This could be done by getting your financial statements in order; by estimating the value of the tangible assets of your business and by preparing your statement of seller's discretionary earnings. Are you able to perform your side of the agreement to the fullest?"

Angela tried to shake off the feeling of oppression that settled over her. A sparkle of anger sprang to life inside her. She had judged him. She had formed her own opinion of him, and decided he was cruel and rude and downright arrogant. He doesn't want to listen to her. He does not consider the dire circumstances she is already facing. He doesn't feel her agony and loss. He gives himself the right to press hard as if he already owns the company. He has a serious "my-way's-the-only-way" attitude. He came here to impose his views on her and take her company away. This person is a potential pain. She hates him. She just hates him.

She shot him an indignant glance and said haughtily, "We have spent so much time dealing with you. I am afraid I have to leave. I have an important appointment."

Angela left the room without saying even goodbye. Her people also left without a word. Hashem was really amazed to see such reckless behaviour on her part. He was extremely offended, he could have given up the deal and gets a better one, but her strange behaviour made him think that she was dangerous and unstable. He wanted to know everything about her.

Hashem went to the secretary and asked her about the important appointment Angela was about to attend. The secretary smiled and said, "She is going to dance."

Hashem asked surprised, "Dance! where?"

"Ball and Chain club." The secretary said smiling.

Hashem drove his porch to Ball and Chain club, and there he saw her dancing alone without a partner. She was wearing black tights and dancing like an angel. He saw her so fragile and so beautiful in that black tights. The music was superb. It was the power of love lyric sang by Luciano Pavarotti. Her graceful dance mesmerized him.

It was more than a dance. He could see that her dance was conveying something very personal. And he was right. She was dreaming alone whispering to herself, "Nobody is going to hurt me here. Here I am safe - safe from everyone."

His gaze roamed her beautiful face, and saw tears rolling down her face. She was weeping while dancing.

Hashem did not know that Angela surrounds herself with a shield as an area of self-privacy and protection. If an intruder enters her space without permission, it makes her feel very uncomfortable and she reacts in some negative way.

After dancing, Angela went to take her car. Hashem met her there, and started a small conversation.

Hashem: "We have to talk. I still have a few questions that need answers. How about tomorrow?

Angela: "Tomorrow is a day off. I spend my holidays on the beach. I want to enjoy sun-soaked without interference please."

Hashem:" But we must talk. I am going home tomorrow."

She said nervously: "I do not discuss business in my day off. I need space. Surely, I am entitled to some privacy if you do not mind.

He looked at her eyes and saw her eyes still wet with her tears.

Hashem: "Why are you so repulsive? I meant well."

"Sorry. I am not good at relationships. I am not fun to be around. I do not fit in." She said looking away trying to escape from his dark penetrating eyes.

She swallowed her tears and got into her car. She drove off before he could respond.

He kept looking at the car until it disappeared around the corner.

"Crazy woman." He muttered.

CHAPTER 3

Angela lay on the beach and soaked up sunshine. Her bikini revealed her beautiful well-proportioned body. After a short while, she sat up, hugging her knees to her chest looking toward the sea.

Unexpectedly, she saw Hashem coming out of the water with his massive muscular body. He bent down and picked up his T-shirt. He then moved towards her with athletic grace. But suddenly he found himself surrounded by a bikini-clad bevy of beauties. The women were throwing themselves at him. They enjoyed touching his bulging biceps and triceps and his well-defined upper and lower abs.

Angela glared at him refusing to lower her gaze marvelling the muscular strength of his perfect body. His arms were massive and bulging with biceps and triceps. His large shoulders were pounded with thick muscles. His chest and stomach were so hard and contoured.

Hashem excused himself with a polite smile, but the girls followed him until he reached Angela.

"We are having a party tonight. You are welcome to join us. Our place isn't far." One of the girls said.

"No thanks. I have other commitments." He smiled and lifted his hand apologizing.

The girls laughed as they made their way down toward the sea.

Omar looked at Angela. She was looking downward unable to look in his eyes, her face reddening with embarrassment. He fell to his knees in the sand before her.

"Look at me." He said in an orderly tone.

She raised her head, and her gaze met his own.

"How dare you speak to me in that tone of voice?" She said angrily.

He ran both hands through his wet hair to push it back. It fascinated her, seeing the water drops trickle down along the deep grooves that etched his chest and abdomen.

Water dripping down his face, he sang, "drip, drip, rain falls giving life, giving hope." down his face, he sang. Seeing his boldness, she became very upset. She glanced at him nervously.

"I want to be let alone. Please do not intrude on my privacy."

"But you need to breathe. You need someone to sit beside you.You are now free to succeed again. It's simple, you see."

"The failure is bigger than you expect." She said with watery eyes.

"Business failure is often just a step on the way to success. Do not lose your risk appetite and take the leap all over again." He said consoling her.

"I feel like a failure. Every failure kills me." She said through her tears.

Her hand shaking commenced and he noticed it.

"My right-hand shakes uncontrollably when I am angry, stressed or tired. I left the pills in the car." She said embarrassed.

He held her hand to stop the tremor.

"Accept your failure and think differently. The more you speak about failure, the easier it will become for you to deal with." He said giving her hand a gentle massage.

To her amazement, she surrendered to his touches and found her body relaxing.

"So, you've made up your mind and you want to give that failing business a try." She said trying to sober up from the sweet effect his touches were making to her stiff body.

"I will not buy you off. We will be partners. To be successful, we will analyse and offer new and innovative ideas to keep the customers coming back. The goal is to make the company's management more effective, improve financing and repay the credit."

"Why do you care about me? Is it out of pity?"

"You are a woman in distress and I want to help."

"Just like that. A woman in distress! A woman you know nothing about. We have only met yesterday."

"Yesterday, I saw you dancing, and weeping. I saw your loneliness and sadness channelled into a silent dance. Because you cannot express your sadness and loneliness, you danced them. I felt your dancing would give you the strength to continue against all odds. In that moment, I felt you need me, and here I am extending my hand to you."

"I was just trying to shatter borders between body, heart and mind." She smiled at him through watery eyes.

"You see, the tremor has stopped. What you need is not drugs, but a man to take care of you. He said releasing her hand.

"I am a complicated woman. I am different. I don't have time for men."

"A little complexity does a person good." He said laughing.

"I am difficult to figure out. I tend to keep more to myself than normal people do."

"You like to surround yourself by an aura of mystery. Many men fall for it. You are also an independent woman. Many men feel more attracted to an independent woman."

"Thank you for the kind words." She faintly smiled.

"Come, let me take you to your car." He said putting over the swim shorts his t-shirt. He covered her with her bath gown, and both strode toward their cars. She sat in her car smiling at him appreciatively.

"We are going to have a small meeting tomorrow at your office. Okay!" he said waving his hand goodbye.

"Okay." She said smiling.

"Nature had squandered an unreasonable quantity of male beauty on this creature." She whispered to herself. This was a person she wanted to know more than she'd ever felt before. She could love this man for eternity. In that moment, she felt her body flush warm.

She liked the way he moves. He walks smoothly like fresh water. She waited to see him walking to his car. He reached his convertible porch and jumped into it. The car roared off in the direction of his hotel.

CHAPTER 4

In Angela's office, Hashem sat with his people confronting Angela and her lawyer. He started to talk:

"The company is failing due to poor management. The company needs money to pay off debts. Advertising is important, especially if it is a failing business. No one will visit our new business if we do not advertise. We will seek the help of local newspaper, radio and television.

"The business also failed because there were no customers. Talking to our customers is essential if we want to succeed. We will get the customer's input on what they would like to see and implement their ideas.

"It is not wise to use our working capital in renovations. Renovations will eat up our working capital fast. We will find ways to revamp our business while keeping the bulk of our working capital intact.

"Instead of buying the company for a low price, I am giving the company an opportunity to grow market share via financial support. Injecting money in this stage can keep the company afloat until problems are solved and the company is restructured. This will help the company continue operating with the same suppliers, employees and customers.

"Hashem then addressed Angela saying, "You have a serious job to do. You will be responsible for all the company's operations segment. You will be responsible for helping to ensure that customers ultimately receive the product or service that the company promises. You will be in charge of the market unit to attract customers and providing production staff with guidance on how to develop and perfect the offering.

"I will send one of my capable accountants to set the company's budget and to ensure that operational capacity is properly managed. I will also send an expert in quality management control. All operational units of a business have to keep quality in mind on a higher level. You must work with suppliers regularly to ensure the best quality product for the most reasonable price possible.

"Angela, you will be also responsible for the administrative unit. It will be responsible of ordering supplies, hiring employees, and managing communication within and outside of the firm.

"Angela, write these ideas down and see which are essential and which ones can wait. Write a good business plan, especially when you need funding. Bad business planning is what makes businesses fail."

Angela: "You scared the hell out of me. I need your help. You can help in every step along the way."

Hashem: "My hand is extended to you. Try your best to stay calm — the coming months are going to be very hard and you'll need to stay focused and level-headed as much as possible."

Angela: "I am concerned about the fate of my team and the possible end of the business they built with their blood, sweat, and tears.'

Hashem: "I do care about your team. Worrying about their future is completely understandable. But when money begins to get tight, one of the first things you are going to need to address is whether or not you'll have to fire anyone. Cuts have to be made, or money is just going to dry up even faster, giving you less time to get your business back on track. However, if things go well, you can always hire them to come back on board.

Hashem: "Angela, are you up to it? Can you fulfil your part of the bargain? If you can't, I am ready to negotiate with you for a Buy It Now Price."

Angela: "I will do my best to keep the company afloat."

Hashem: "I will split the profits 80% for me and 20% for you. Is that okay with you?

Angela: "Yes. You will be paying a lot to rescue the company from ruin."

Hashem: "Good girl. I may increase your profit share in the future, if you bring profits back to a higher level. Now let us finalize the agreement. Your lawyer and my lawyer will sit together to wrap things up, and conclude the bargain."

"Will you excuse me gentlemen I have an important meeting to attend." Hashem said suddenly and left the room in haste.

She was surprised to see him leaving so soon without even saying goodbye. He left quickly like a passing cloud. He was a mystery to her. He is the leader here. Obviously, his skills were far superior to her. He could have bought her company with a small price, but he preferred to be a partner! He is a strong man and is able to protect her. She wants that man in her life.

She was amazed to see herself whispering to her soul, "I don't think I could fit into your life. I am a loner, not your beloved. How I long to be your woman – your only woman."

CHAPTER 5

In that very night, in her bed, she thought a lot about Hashem. His perfect muscular body excited her. She wanted to touch his muscular chest and flat abs. He was such a wild beautiful creature to see. He was without a doubt the sexiest man she had ever seen.

She has never felt sexually attracted to men. She was happy being single, but when he knelt down very close to her and looked intently in her eyes, her heart flopped in her chest. This wild beautiful creature has awakened her dormant sexuality. He incited in her that feeling of wanting to be filled so badly that it hurts. Suddenly and unexpectedly, she felt this warm wetness splash inside of her. She wanted him, bad, so bad she ached for him, felt empty without him. She wanted him to fill the void in her life.

His views about restructuring the company and the duties he imposed on her were arrogant and domineering, but also financially logic and productive.

Hashem is a strong influential man able to protect her. She wants that man in her life. She must own him, like every other thing she owned before!

Hashem decided to stay in the United States for a couple of months to see the improvement Angela is going to make to rescue the failing company. He wanted to be sure that Angela could generate positive cash flow that would be sufficient to settle debts, pay expenses and provide a buffer against future financial challenges.

Based on the principles Hashem pointed out for the reviving of the company, in addition to the sufficient funding the company received from him, Angela decided to restructure the company to become more market-oriented. She announced the changes at a meeting. She gave a short speech outlining the general reasons for the new company orientation.

She highlighted the fundamental business/strategic problem that her company faces. Among the points she emphasised that she decided to lay-off dozens of employees and set a quick timetable for the layoffs.

Angela wanted to discuss with Hashem the restructuring plan of the company and the factors that determine its success.

She called Hashem for an appointment, he told her that he had an appointment at 7pm and he will meet her at the hotel lobby at 8pm.

Angela parked her car in the hotel garage when a dark-skinned male with a stocky build opened her door and pulled her from the vehicle. He held her from behind, she tried to scream but he put his hand over her mouth.

Shut up, you miserable selfish bitch. You treated me unfairly. Why did you fire me? You think I am defective or something." The assailant said while cupping her chests from behind.

Angela tried to reason with him, "Your termination from the company has nothing to do with your value as a person."

"You ruined me when you laid me off. I have family to keep. I have made personal sacrifices, worked a lot of overtime and flexible hours over the years. You left me out in the cold world. You made me feel less self-worth and made me doubt myself." He said while kissing her back neck and the side of her cheek.

"It is not personal, it is business. This is strict business." She said feeling suffocated.

"Stop talking Chiquita banana, chicken hoe. I want to taste you. I want to bury myself inside you." He said pressing hard against her buttocks. She felt his hardness against her and that maddened her further. She fiercely struggled to release herself from his firm grasp but his arms tightened strongly about her preventing her to move freely. Angela felt extremely angry and began to scream at the aggressor, "You are a good for nothing scoundrel. Go fuck yourself cunt face."

She kicked back to wrench herself from the strong hold the aggressor had on her body, but he pushed her to a wall and pressed hard against her back. Her head hit the wall and a gasp escaped her lips. She tried again to pull away but to no avail.

"Do not resist bitch. I am going to have my way with you and I am going to make you enjoy it. I am going to make you my whore." His voice was hoarse.

"Get away from me, piece of shit, shit fucker." She said trying to disengage herself from his grip. She felt tears welling up in her eyes and she began sobbing.

As the assailant was holding Angela's back, a hand caught at his shoulder. The assailant turned around to receive cruel strike sliced across his face that left his cheeks singing and his nose feeling as though it had been buried in the back of his head. Blood oozed over his mouth and chin. The man hit him in the stomach with a fist that felt like a lump of steel. The assailant crumpled, and sank toward the ground. The man did not let him get up, he took a step back and launched two strong kicks that crashed against the side of the assailant's body.

The assailant was not able to get up, so the man knelt swiftly and grabbed a handful of the assailant's hair, yanking him to his feet, and then started punching him hard in the stomach and chest until the assailant fail unconscious on the ground.

Angela looked at the rescuer to see Hashem's face flushed red with anger as he glared down at the assailant with bulging eyes. The assailant looked like he might pass out.

"Hashem, stop, you are going to kill him." Angela said startled.

"I get really angry when I see a woman being attacked."

He glanced at her, she was trembling all over. Her hand was shaking convulsively.

"Come." He grabbed her hand and both made their way through the elevator and into his hotel suite.

She stood in the middle of the Royal suite marvelling its lavishly interiors, majestic colour scheme and sumptuous furnishings.

"My bathroom is over there. Take a shower." He said in an orderly tone.

She said annoyed. "I do not need a shower."

"You peed out of fright. You got soaked all down your legs; your clothes are wet".

She looked down at her feet and saw them wet. She felt extremely embarrassed.

"After bathing get your clothes together for laundry. You will find the laundry basket in the bathroom."

"What clothes will I wear?"

"You can use my bathrobe.

Angela turned the shower on and stood underneath the flowing water that was running down her body. She rinsed the perfumed soap from her body and wrapped herself in the bathrobe. She got out of the bath to see Hashem sitting on a couch reading a book. She sat down on a chair opposite him looking at him.

Hashem called room service, "Could you send someone up to pick up some laundry? I want it ready in an hour please."

Five minutes later, a man from room service came and took the laundry for wash and dry cleaning.

Hashem wore jeans and a snug t-shirt that outlined his muscular frame. The sight of his dishevelled hair, the gorgeous spread of his shoulders, tapering down to the narrow thrust of his hips, made her ovaries ache deep in her belly. All of his beauties are meant to be touched. She wanted to run her hand through his body.

"Was that man who abused you one of your employees?" He asked.

"Yes. He was laid off just recently." I truly cared for all of my employees and when I had to lay people off for business reasons, I cry because it really hurt to do that."

"How many times must I rescue you from trouble?"

"I am sorry for all the trouble I have brought you."

"They say you are an independent woman, but I see you weak and vulnerable."

"I have an incredible sense of self because I am so in touch with who I am and who I want to be."

"So you do not need help from men?"

"No. My pride is mighty, and I will do anything to avoid swallowing it. I am able to wiggle my way out of sticky situations with absolute ease."

"Oh! But you needed help from a man to revive your failing company!"

"This is another story. The failing of companies is due to a worldwide financial crisis."

"It is also due to incompetent management, lack of funds, poor marketing, separation between producers and consumers. Your company suffered from all these shortages. You even needed a man to save you from a violent attack by a man who physically abused you. A lady in continuous distress, that's what you are." He said numbering her shortfalls.

"Your employees complain that you have a haughty and domineering temper." He said eager to know her response.

"I have a natural talent to influence people. I like to have authority over people. Modesty does not become me. I find it easy to manipulate people." She said in a matter of fact manner.

She reached into her handbag, took out of a cigarette, and lit it using a slim gold lighter which she dropped back into her bag. She drew on her cigarette hard, throwing her head back, she let the smoke curl gently out of her nostrils.

She said through the smoke of her cigarette, "I've got so used to being on my own. I was always aware I couldn't be a full part of the normal lives other people were having. Therefore, in many ways I felt a loner. However, the most real part of me is intimate, passionate and generous, and I need to be in a relationship for that to come out."

He paused for a moment contemplating her - a beautiful arrogant woman sitting before him in his bathrobe showing off her fine sexy legs. He liked her light brown hair, her hazel eyes, and full lips.

"You said you do not need help from men. Do you like men? Do you feel anything towards them?" He said looking straight into her eyes.

"I have never had any desires or needs for sex. I have never felt that drive, that impulse, to partake in sex. It is not that I find it repulsing; it's not that I find it boring either, it's just that there is no bodily impulse or drive for it. The fact that I am not experiencing sexual attraction tells me that I am Asexual."

"I find you a very attractive woman. You just haven't experienced sex yet, when you do you might change your mind."

She did not answer him, but looked at him smiling.

"You are a very strange woman. You called the man who assaulted you foul disgusting names. You are a horrible nasty person. You are weirdo."

She said laughing aloud, "My employees call me "foul-mouthed ruffian."

"How do you see me, another ruthless aggressive man?" He said wonderingly.

"I see you a very emotional person, but your emotions go out of the window when you take crucial decisions in business or in your personal life."

"Can I tell you something? But please do not get me wrong." She said straightening herself up in her seat.

"Go ahead."

"I am very much attracted to you."

"Oh!"

"You have triggered all my sexual instincts and desires."

"And when that happened?"

"When I saw you in the beach, when you offered help, when you loved my dancing, when you saved me from the assailant, and when you proposed a shower to become beautiful in your eyes."

"You are a bold daring woman I am afraid."

"Do you think I am beautiful?" She said with an inviting smile on her face.

"You are beautiful, but so what? Beautiful women are everywhere."

"Oh! You think so." She said rising from her seat. She untied the belt of the bathrobe, opened it and let it fall to the floor, displaying her naked body to him.

Hashem was stunned. The sight of her body was almost dizzying, perfect features, perfect body. Angela's naked body was just delicious, so exquisitely shaped, so perfectly made, so lithe and yet so charmingly rounded and plump, so juicy and fresh, so virgin! She stood before him lithe, graceful with exquisite curves.

His eyes widened at her bold move. "Are you nuts?" He shouted at her.

He rose from the couch and walked towards her. "Come back to your senses please." He said picking up the robe and wrapping it around her naked body.

"It's just me throwing myself at you." She said putting her hands around his neck and brought her lips to his. He tried to tear himself away from her but she held him tighter. He felt a strong heat rising in his body.

"You've got an awfully kissable mouth." She said enjoying the kiss.

His breath grew warm from her kiss. Touching her set him to flame.

"I am lusting over you." She said with a smile playing at her lips.

"I am hard to love. He said trying to escape temptation.

"Oh! Don't give me that." She said while continuing kissing him.

"I could kiss your lips all night long if you just let me." She said enjoying his warm lips.

"Sober up and stop this nonsense." He said in a harsh tone.

"I just want to rip your clothes off so bad. I ache for you."

He tried to liberate himself but she gripped him tightly.

"What are you afraid of? I promise I will not burn you." Her lips tightened further.

Holding her body against his chest made him very much aware of her as a woman. Her lips were soft and pliant. He felt his rising lust, the rising heat.

Quivering all over, he disengaged himself firmly from her body.

She glanced up at him as if he were God Himself.

"Make love to me." She begged.

"In our religion, there is no sex outside marriage."

"Then marry me please."

"I have no time for women. I am not the marrying type."

"We can make a great match; we can have a happy marriage."

"No thank you I am fine."

She laughed aloud and kissed his chest.

"Please reconsider." She said caressing his cheek.

"The only way I'd lay naked with you would be in a mass grave."

She gave him a coquettish smile, leaned forward and kissed his lips.

The laundryman knocked on the door. Hashem opened the door for him and took the clean clothes.

"Now put your clothes on and leave." He said pointing out to his bedroom.

She went to his bedroom and put her clothes on.

"Thank you for the lovely night." She said with a sorrowful look.

She stopped at the door, turned back and glanced at him. He drowned in the sweetest desire of her warm gaze.

"Even before we met and long after we're both gone, my heart lives inside of yours. I am forever and ever in love with you. I am your woman, and you are my man. You will marry me. And I know you will be a good father and husband."

He said to change the subject, "I have night-time tea, it really helps you get to sleep. Do you want some?"

"No thanks." She said walking to the door.

He did not want her to leave. He did not want her to stay either.

"Do you have to leave so soon? I was just about to poison the tea." He said mockingly.

She laughed merrily and ran to him, kissed his cheek and hugged him. She then strode to the door, opened it, went out and closed it behind her.

He stood looking at the closed door. This combination of beauty and boldness amazed him. Although she was an independent woman, she does not feel safe on her own. She was attracted to him because he would keep her safe under any circumstance. He wanted to calm her fears, fill the void of her loneliness, and protect her from the vicissitudes of life.

He saw her so deliciously vulnerable. She kissed him and awakened his sexual desire. He felt a strong desire to possess her and make her wholly his.

CHAPTER 6

Angela called Hashem on the phone and invited him to have tea with her mother.

"Your mother! What a bad idea."

"You are damned right. She is fat, nasty, and obnoxious." She said laughing.

"You certainly derive from a very good family." He said mocking.

"How about picking you up at 7pm?"

"No thank you. I don't like the idea of seeing your mother."

"I want you to see the other side of me."

"What other side?"

"The side of Jealousy, insecurity, arrogance, etc."

"Don't drag me to your personal life please."

"I want you to know everything about me."

"Sorry, I am not interested."

"You must be interested because I want you to be mine. You are going to fall in love with me."

"You don't own me; I am not just one of your many toys."

"Please Hashem, it's a day off, stay away from routine, get some fresh air."

"Get some fresh air with your mother! Are you crazy?"

Please Hashem, changing the work mood is probably one of the most beautiful things people can do."

He said after long hesitation, "Okay, come at seven."

Angela picked Hashem up at his hotel at 7pm in her convertible BMW. Hashem climbed into the car beside her and placed his arm protectively on the back of the seat behind her neck. It amazed him to see that she was driving the car bare foot, her high heel shoes were placed on the car seat next to her.

"You amaze me. You are always mysterious and unpredictable." He said admiring her Nefertiti face profile.

"I am just being myself. I am comfortable with who I am."

Angela wanted to give Hashem a brief about her mother, so she talked while driving:

"I grew up with an overweight mother. Her family is obnoxious and is complete trash. They are all overweight with horrible eating habits and alcoholism. My mother is very loud and likes to embarrass people and call them out in front of as big of an audience as possible. She made it her mission to embarrass me whenever possible."

"O! I am sorry to hear that."

"She always treated me like shit. When I was a child she hit me enough to leave marks that caused me so much misery."

"Is she emotionally crippled?"

"I have learnt, from my father, that she is mentally disturbed, and is a product of her hostile upbringing. She is allergic to reality. If there is something she did not like then she simply ignores it. My mother ignored me. If I did something that I thought would make her proud, she would either dismiss it as insignificant or undercut it in some other way. She never listens to me or hears me."

"She is narcissist then!"

"Call her a narcissist if you wish. The tactics she uses to manipulate and control me permit her to self-aggrandize and feel good about herself. I have no relationship with my mother; to her I am just a gold mine."

"Do you hate her? I hope not."

"I feel shame that I came from this disgusting and dumb woman. I do not hate her. I pity her."

"And what about your father?"

"My father was a brilliant person, clever, successful, and charismatic - a prominent industrialist. He taught me how to be a good entrepreneur. He was a tough man and taught me the value of money. Even today, when I run the company I think of him whenever I have to take crucial financial decisions. I love my father and I appreciate him so much. You remind me of him."

Angela parked her car in front of a grand villa. She rang the bell; a black servant opened the door. He led them to the living room where her mother was sitting on an electric wheel chair waiting for them. Angela bent forward and kissed her mother, she then introduced Hashem to her mother saying, "This is Hashem – a good friend." Hashem nodded smiling, and sat close to Angela on a couch opposite her mother.

The mother was so fat that she could not walk by herself. The electric wheel chair was a transportation device that would make her move with ease.

The mother examined Hashem from head to foot. She then looked at Angela saying, "Where did you find this very good-looking man? Was it in a bar or a nightclub? Ha..Ha..Ha." The mother laughed hysterically.

"Mother, please behave." Hashem is a decent man. We run a business together." Angela said embarrassed.

The mother looked at Hashem as if he were stupid. She then said, "The problem with Angela is that she hates men, she hates being touched by men. I always advised her to go to bars and nightclubs to pick up men and bring them home, but she did not listen to me. She is stubborn like her father."

"Mama please." Angela said annoyed.

"The problem with you Angela is that you have not tasted men before, if you taste them you will overcome your inferiority complex."

The black servant came with tea and cakes. Hashem and Angela sipped tea and took tiny bites out of the cakes.

The mother looked at Hashem and said, "What did you see in Angela that made you like her?"

"She is a fine lady, and a successful business woman."

"She needs to be laid, I am telling you. This will calm her and ease her nerves."

Instantly, the mother fell asleep snoring loudly.

"Let's go." Angela said, standing.

Angela drove the car in silence. She looked at Hashem and inquired,

"How did you see my old tart?"

"What do you mean by old tart?" He said curious to inquire the meaning of the word.

"My mother." She said with a mocking smile.

Her obscene words embarrassed him. "I would never think you would say something like that about your mother. He said annoyed.

"I am sorry." She said quickly as if unwilling to admit her mistake.

"No, really I mean it. What do you think about my mother?" She repeated her inquiry.

Although he disapproved her ill behaviour, her impudence intrigued him. He kept silent for a moment examining her sensuous body, and then his unexpected answer came like a laughing bomb.

"Your mama so fat when she jumps up in the air she gets stuck." Angela burst out laughing,

"You are so funny, you really make me laugh."

"Your mama is so fat the government shut her down along with the rest of the national parks." He shot another laughing bomb.

She laughed her heart out. "You make me laugh until my ribs hurt. O God. I love you, I love you." She said slapping her knees. "

She drove laughing uncontrollably. "But you are nothing like your mom." He said happy to see her laughing so heartily.

"Her painful fat condition inspired me to stay fit and take care of myself." She said through her laughter.

"So what's the next place, where do we go from here?" Hashem demanded.

"How about dancing." She said with a cheerful smile.

He laughed. "Dance is the hidden language of the soul. Yes, let's dance."

"Yes, my love. Let the dancing flow!"

They reached the dance club. They sat down at a table set for two. They ordered ice tea. They sipped the ice tea listening to the slow tango La Comparsita.

"Do you know how to dance?" She asked smiling like a playful cat.

"Yes I do. I have danced with many women before."

Angela's smirk that had been on her face slowly had changed into a frown of jealousy. She felt anxious and insecure - her relationship with him is under threat.

"Were they beautiful?" She asked in a jealous tone.

"I only dance with beautiful women." He said noticing her sudden jealousy.

A sign of displeasure showed on her face.

"Are you jealous of women you didn't even know?" He said in concern.

"I am jealous because I didn't share that time with you.'

"Why do you like to dance?" She said trying to change the subject.

"It tones my body and keeps me physically fit."

"So you think you can dance with me?"

"I am reasonably good at most partner dances, but I do not know if I am the ideal partner for you."

"Just take my hand, I will spin you around, will not let you fall down. Would you let me lead?"

"You want to teach me to dance! All you can do is swim in my moves and drink my essence." He said sure of himself.

She laughed giggly watching his hypnotic eyes coupled with raw sex appeal.

A mix of Salsa, Mambo and Merengue music started to play through a powerful PA system. They looked around in pleasure.

"Shall we dance? Come on let's have some fun." She took his hand in hers and moved to the dance floor.

They danced beautifully together with warm and passion. Hashem was a smooth, confident dancing partner. His expertise made her look graceful in his arms. They geared around each other and made many beautiful spins, twists and turns. They made knot combinations, and then separated to perform individual moves. They transformed themselves into energetic, healing, delightful moving forms.

The music turned into Bachata dance, a very beautiful and sensual dance, the rhythm is different from Salsa. It is easier than salsa in some way. They moved their bodies in a way that was simply jaw dropping.

When the music played Kizomba dance, a very sexy dance in which the couple is very close. They danced with the hips touching and arms around each other. Their movement was fluid and sensual. They danced without moving their feet, just moving their hips together in time with the music.

He enjoyed the feeling of Angela in his arms as they moved to the rhythm of the Kizomba music.

Her legs felt like jelly, and he was glistening with sweat. She started to get a sense of pain and pleasure.

As close as they were, a surge of desire rushed through him, and found himself with a strong male reaction, Angela felt it too. She gazed up at him with misty eyes and dropped a small kiss on his lips.

"It is so wonderful feeling your arms Wrapped around my body. I just got lost with you. You're what I want, come and get me." She whispered in his eyes.

The music stopped and they left the dance floor.

"Could you drop me at my hotel?" He said in an absent tone. He was deep in some strong emotions whirling in his head.

She drove in silence. She did not want to wake up from the strong feeling she felt while dancing with him. She felt wonderful and alive. His formidable dancing astounded her. He danced like a pro. Dancing with him was like a journey of the soul to freedom through the releasing of her heart, mind and body. The magic she was feeling was not the music, but was contained solely within his arms. He made her soul wanted to flee to a brighter horizon.

Does he know the effect he is having on her? She wondered.

She dropped him off at his hotel.

"Why don't you join me for dinner tomorrow in my sweet?" He said while getting out of the car.

"I would love to." She said happily with a sweet smile on her face.

CHAPTER 7

The chef prepared a private candle light dinner for two in Hashem's sweet. Candle light filled the room as soft music whispered in the background.

Hashem looked great in a black tie tuxedo. His shirt featured mother of pearl buttons. Angela wore a V- neck black short dress revealing her sexy long legs. In her neck was a necklace, its red gem 'sparkling' in the candle light. Her hair in the candle light danced like a flame.

Mushroom chicken picatta was served with brown rice and steamed green beans. Grilled Caesar salad was served with low fat dressing. The dessert was banana pudding topped with whipped cream.

They chatted while eating.

Hashem: "Close your eyes and make a wish with the purest intentions."

She closed her eyes for long seconds and then opened her eyes smiling at him.

"What did you wish for?" He demanded.

"I wished you could be mine."

"You should never wish for wishful thinking."

"You are my dear love. I will do anything to keep you."

"I am not the marrying kind. Business is my life. I do not want to be shackled by marriage. I want to be free."

"I wish you could understand the way I feel about you." Her eyes held a glint of sadness.

"Do not smash yourself to bits on the rocks."

"How can I be more pleasant to your eyes?"

"You are a good-looking woman pleasant to the eyes."

"So what's the problem? I'll be your sunshine, you can be mine."

"There is no future in it. There are many miles between us."

"But still our souls can meet. Don't you feel the need for someone to come into your life?" She said with fresh tears spilling from her eyes.

"I know I am a woman with shortfalls. I am narcissist, jealous, weird and contemptuous. I also suffer from neurological disease." She said sobbing.

"O Angela, please take it easy." He said grieved.

"You are the only man who awakened my sexual desires. You are the only man who made me feel like a natural woman. Without you, I am lost. Save me from the scars."

His heart ached to see her in such pain. He reached for her hand and gave it a reassuring squeeze.

"I love you, marry me." She said wiping out her tears.

"Please try to understand. Marriage is a serious matter. Always be the woman a man needs, not the woman who needs a man. A wife shows submission unto her husband when she allows him to take leadership in the relationship. Submission should not be confused with a person being weak. Your nature refuses to submit unto man. Your nature is combative and firm. If I marry you, you will turn my life into a living hell I am sure."

She rose from her seat at the table. "let's dance." She said stretching out her hand to him, as if dancing would relief her from anxiety and stress.

She flung her arms around him and pressed her face against his chest. They danced to the tango music playing in the background.

She wanted to feel his body pressed against hers, wanted to touch all of him.

"I do not want to go back to my lonely deprived life. I want to know what love is, I know you can show me what love is." She looked up at his wide black eyes and kissed his lips gently. A delightful little shiver ran through his body.

"Men love a sane woman. Your bad habits and toxic attitudes could ruin any marriage. Living with me, isn't going to change the root causes of your life attitudes." He said enjoying the scent of her sweet perfume.

"I inherited these bad habits from mom. She used to call me harsh and derogatory words: 'Get the fuck out of my sight, weak piece of shit, fuck you." She said laughing aloud.

"You are a foul-mouthed woman. I hate insolent words. Be rational and sensible please. You're so much smarter when you don't speak!" A little smile played on his face.

"I'm selfish, impatient and jealous. I make mistakes, I am out of control and at times hard to handle. I wish I could be what you want but I cannot and I'm sorry.

"Try Angela, please try." He said sincerely.

"I could never be like you. I have a heart." She said looking up at him with misty eyes.

"I don't get how you could be that fucked up to someone who really cares about you." She said through her tears.

"We said no obscene words. You are pissing me off. I'm so fucking fed up with you." He said irritated.

"Take care with your words mister, this is offensive language." She laughed hilariously.

"I don't know what happened to me, but what the fuck?" He laughed until tears rolled from his eyes.

"O shit! I love this. I love that you be your own self." She said clinging to his neck and laughing merrily.

He looked down at her. He brushed back her hair and pressed his lips against hers. Her lips were soft and sweet. She placed her arms around his neck. He kissed her harder, his tongue exploring her mouth thoroughly. She deepened her kiss, savouring his lips against hers. He pulls away moving his fiery kisses down her neck. Heat surged through him and settled in his groin. His kisses stirred the hot embers of her passion into flame. He then felt her hands moving down his chest, coming to a stop at the top of his trousers. He moved back.

"Please, don't." He started breathing hard.

"Why not? That is what a man does when he loves a woman. Comfort her, ease her sorrows, and fulfil the desires of her passion."

"Angela, please try to understand. You are a very beautiful woman and you excite me a lot, but we are cut from two different cultures. You do not belong to my world."

"How is that?" She said sobbing.

"In our tradition, the task of a wife is to love and respect her husband. The prosperity and happiness as well as the misery of the family are in her hands. It is not an easy undertaking. A man's highest need is to feel respect."

"And you think I may not make a good wife?"

"Sorry Angela, a woman like you can easily turn my life into a burning hell."

"I could be a good wife because I love you."

"Believe me Angela, there is no future in it. You have bad traits that would ruin my life."

"What traits?" She said wiping out her tears.

"You are bossy, vulgar, jealous, and short-tempered."

"What else do you have against me?" She said downhearted.

"You are crazy in all the wrong ways."

"Love can heal the scars and wounds, you know."

"I am sorry Angela, please try to understand." He said nervously trying to end the conversation.

"The only problem with you is that you are too perfect. I like flaws; I think they make things interesting." She said lifting his hand to her lips and kissing it.

"I am not an angel, and I will not be one till I die: I will be myself." She said wetting his hand with her tears.

"The one who truly loved me will see beyond my flaws, embrace me in spite of them, and love me through them." She lifted his other hand and kissed it then put both hands on her cheeks.

She looked in his eyes and said with a sad smile, "I am full of flaws, but they are stitched together with good intentions."

"Good intentions do not always solve problems." He said feeling a tremendous pity for her.

"This is what I am, and this is what I want to be with you." She said through a tearful smile.

"I may be imperfect today, but with you I will strive every day to become just a little better. You will ignore my weakness and cover my scars."

Her words crushed his heart. The sincerity of her genuine honesty broke what was left of his ego. A tear dropped from his eye.

She wiped it away with her delicate finger and said, "The best love is the one that makes you a better person, without changing you into someone other than yourself. Your love, patience, and wisdom will heal me little by little."

He looked deeply into her eyes, and saw her vulnerability and weakness. He could feel his need to comfort her, to protect her from every ounce of pain or danger.

"I am leaving tomorrow." He said.

"When are you coming back?"

"I don't think I will be. I have finished my work here."

She started crying and trembling all over. He held her tight to smooth her pain away.

"It hurts too much not to be with you. You are the pain that I won't give up." She said weeping.

She kissed his lips, broke away from his arms, and then strolled to the door. She stopped at the door and turned back to face him.

"Thank you for the most delicious dinner I ever had. You broke my heart but I still love you with all the pieces. I will always be yours even if you do not want me." She opened the door and walked out with a sad heart.

CHAPTER 8

Hashem sat in his private jet heading to the Emirates. Thoughts whirled in his mind. He does not belong here; he belongs to a more conservative world.

In his world, women must obey their husbands and take care of them. And this does not belittle them, but it provides energy to make a better family life. It is a job requiring sagacity, style, and ingenuity. For a woman to be a successful wife, she should win over her husband's heart and be a source of comfort to him.

But what about Angela - a woman full of flaws and contradictions. If she enters his life with her shortcomings, she would surely ruin it.

Six months had passed but her memory lingered in the back of his mind too fresh to let go as if it happened yesterday. He tried desperately to forget her but he could recall every detail.

What intrigued him so much in her? Was it her average brown hair, her conventional pretty face, or her correct female figure? There is nothing remarkable in fact!

He knew he had to go over her, to clear his mind in preparation for the hard work that lay ahead of him, but he was intoxicated by the moments he spent with her. He wished to forget her, but he knew he never would.

"Let's be realistic", he whispered to himself. She does not fit for a wife. She is awkward and imperfect. She had flaws that would scare men away, but these scary flaws were the things that attracted him most to her. He loved her boldness and honesty. He loved her softness and vulnerability. All her vulnerability was there for him to see. He liked her weakness; he saw her as a withering flower deprived of the sun.

He appreciated her courage in reaching out boldly to him despite her own abandonment. She tasted sweet and innocent to him as he took her in his arms. He loved her warm smile and fluttery laugh, and the clear dewdrops of her eyes that seared his heart. When he buried his nose in her brown hair, breathing in the scent of her hair perfume, this was where he belonged.

She was afraid of men and hated them. She declared herself asexual until she met him. He was the first man in her life. He opened the flood - gates of passion and sexual desires in her. He removed the walls of protection standing between her and her reality, and made her look at him in a different way. When he took her in his arms, his heart melted, and desire exploded through his body. She danced her sadness in silence like a tender dream, and on La Salsa strong rhythm, she danced like a devil.

She wanted him to accept her as she is. She did not even pretend that she would change herself into a good woman for him, so if he wants her, he should take her as she is with all her flaws. She is a free independent woman made entirely of flaws. He loved her simple acceptance of her shortcomings. She was bad in a way that entices, and vulnerable in a way that needs his protection.

The amazing thing is that her flaws were the reason he was falling in love with her. That is why he liked her - because she was crazy - simply unforgettable."

"Nothing is perfect. We all have flaws, and so our love will be flawed." He whispered to himself.

She wanted him – only him. He will have her. He will make her his. He will cleanse her and make her whole.

In Florida, Angela was having a meeting with the heads of departments in the meeting room. The door of the meeting room suddenly opened and Angela saw Hashem standing there smiling. He had an ecstatic smile on his face. He was in a casual beige suit and a white-collar shirt revealing his hairy massive chest. He looked gorgeous to her. Like a baby girl who found her beloved toy, she rushed from her chair to embrace him, but she realized that the head of departments were looking at her and him in amazement. She looked at them annoyed and ordered, "Get lost." They however did not move quickly to leave the meeting room, so she shouted at them again, "I said get lost…you punks."

They took her insulting impertinence with well-bred indifference, and left the room eager to know what was going to happen between their boss and the billionaire who saved her company from ruin.

Angela ran to Hashem, flung her arms around his neck, and fluttered hundreds of kisses across his face.

"Why are you here?" She said looking into his wide black eyes and holding him firmly from his jacket's lapels. Tears of joy streamed down her face.

"You still have a foul mouth. You asked your employees to get lost and called them punks!" He said laughing at her impudence.

"I can't help being sometimes stuck in bad patterns of behaviour. I am nasty to the people who work for me. I can be very abusive and curt. I have an incredible temper and I lash out at everyone."

"You didn't answer my question, why are you here?" She said in an insistent voice.

"I am here because I love you. I did not want to, but it happened."

She stared at him unable to believe her ears, she then burst out,

"You love me? Do you really mean it?"

"Will you marry me?" He said kissing her lips and eyes.

"Marry you? O God!"

She looked at him and could not control her emotions. She laughed merrily with joy, then wept in his arms a river of tears, and he held her while crying.

She felt an uncontrollable urge to pee. She freed herself from his arms and said pointing to a bathroom joined to the meeting room, "I suffer involuntary urination when stressed or exhilarated. It will take only a second. Do not go away please."

She came back after a few moments, her mouth opened in amazement.

"Do you love me? Do you really love me?"

"Yes, I do love you?"

"How did you know that you truly love me?"

"During the past few weeks I lived for those moments when we were together. I began to wonder how long you had been on my mind. Then it occurred to me, since I met you, you have never left."

"I am a woman of flaws. I might cause you harm."

"I am aware of your flaws. I am aware of all the insecurities that you have."

"Could you embrace me for all that I am?"

"I want you, all of you; your flaws, your mistakes, your imperfections, every wicked bit of you."

"I want to love and be loved. Could you be my warmth, my light?"

"I'll be your light, if you will be mine."

"Since you left me things has never been the same. I saw you in every passing moment. The way you looked, the way you danced, the words you said, the things we laughed at. True love comes once in a lifetime, and I have found my love. Yes, my love I will marry you. I will be yours until eternity."

They cradled and wept tears of love and joy.

In order for Hashem to marry Angela, it had to be according to the Sharia law. It is prohibited in the Sharia Law for an unmarried man and woman to live together or share a closed space. Marriage is the only legal bond for a man and a woman to establish a relationship and have children. Hashem and Angela flew on his private jet to Dubai where they registered their marriage in a Sharia court. They used the court's decorated wedding room for few photographs before they proceeded to their wedding party.

The wedding was held in Atlantis The Palm in Dubai. The wedding was attended by 300 guests from around the world.

Now the time has come that Hashem takes her in his arms and teaches her what truly love is. He is the only man in the world with whom she can develop intimacy and surrender completely without holding back. He is the only man whom she could welcome his touches without restraint or shame. She wanted to prove to herself that she was not a failure as a woman. She wanted to experience that rush of sensual pleasure and release.

Their first night together was in the spacious bedroom of Hashem's super yacht. To Angela it was a memorable night. In that night, they felt the depth, the delight and the ecstasy of their life together. Because she was virgin and had no experience with men, she was afraid that Hashem might hurt her. When he wrapped her in his arms, she whispered in his ear, "Love me gently."

Hashem was cordial and patient with her and gave her body the time it needed to respond. He treated her as if she were the only one in the world who mattered. He leaned over and kissed her gently.

"Please let me take good care of you." He whispered while taking her gently in his arms. She closed her eyes and let him do whatever he wanted. He brought his mouth down to her, kissing her gently on her lips. His hands roamed her body and she felt his pleasure in touching her. His kisses became more demanding and his hands roamed over her voluptuous body. Angela grinned and enjoyed his touches. She could not think or speak.

Never had she imagined feeling this way. She had been cold, so very cold, for so very long, and now she was warm, bathed in fire. His perfect body fascinated her. His heat, his smell, his taste, the very essence of him, consumed her.

Her skin caught fire beneath his touches. Desire, long dormant, rose like a fury, curling through her womb and spreading outward like a wildfire. She shivered uncontrollably against him. She yearned to taste him.

"Oh Hashem my love, I am tired of wasting my time being a good girl, with you I want to let loose, please take me, Show me what love really means." She whispered wantonly.

He gathered her in his arms, his lips brushing hers. He deepened his kiss and she grew wetter and hotter. She moaned and basked in the fury of his passion. He drove her mad with his strong strokes. Spasm after spasm worked her body causing her to shudder from the inside out. She clutched to him, burrowing her lips against his neck, her fingers digging into his back.

After what seemed an eternity of strong thrusts, he burst in pleasurable release. Her whole body jumped as she cried out joy of release. She was hungry, so very hungry for more, every piece in her body tingled with delight only to begin a second arousal and a wondrous repetition of sexual vigour she thought was all but dead to her.

He made love to her repeatedly, night after night, telling her that he found her irresistible. The fact that he just could not stop having sex with her delighted her.

Hashem felt he was losing himself to her. He knew he had never felt this before and would never feel it again with any other.

When desire has subsided, he rolled away but held her in his arms covering her lips, cheeks and neck with his kisses until she fell asleep. He watched her for some time until finally, exhausted, he followed her into slumber.

CHAPTER 9

The next morning Angela awoke in the bright sunlight pouring from the window. "Good morning beautiful. What great moments we had last night." Hashem said with a broad smile on his face.

She curled an arm around his neck and pulled him back to her lips. She kissed him a long kiss. "I am planning to make you addicted to me so you couldn't think of another woman." She said seriously.

"Oh! How dominating you are?" He said smiling.

"You are mine. I will possess you. I will own you. And you will never know another woman than me."

"Do not fear other women. I love you. I will always be loyal to you. Now let us have a nice breakfast on deck.

They had a nice freshly prepared breakfast served on deck. Angela was amazed to see that the yacht was already sailing. Starting in Dubai, the Yacht sailed with stops in Salalah, Aqaba, Sharm El Sheikh, Suez Canal, Port Said, Dardanelles, Istanbul, Athens, Valletta, Valencia, and Southampton. The trip took twenty days. From England they flew back in Hashem's private jet to Dubai. In Dubai, they went for sightseeing. They took a helicopter tour over Dubai, and admired the spectacular sights of Dubai from the skies. They soar above the Palm Jumeirah, Burj Al-Arab and Burj Khalifa and other landmarks. They enjoyed spectacular views of Dubai's skyscrapers, beaches and architectural wonders.

From a hot-air balloon, they enjoyed viewing the vast expanse of golden sand dunes, roaming camels, galloping gazelles and the mighty Arabian Oryx in their natural habitat. They were driven to a private desert conservation reserve where they had the chance to freshen up at clean, private bathrooms. Breakfast was a scrumptious selection of delicacies such as hand-cut smoked salmon and caviar.

Hashem and Angela enjoyed a mix of sightseeing and relaxing. They bathed in the open seas enjoying the clear warm coloured blue turquoise water. They walked and lay on the sandy beaches enjoying sunbath.

She asked him, "What did you see in me that made you love me?"

"You are a special fragrance I love to inhale."

His words were sweet to her heart, and rejoiced her soul.

They stayed in his mansion for a month enjoying their intimate relationship. He was hungry for her and she was hungry for him. Every part of him excited her. The more excited she became, the more she kissed every part of him greedily. Her mouth was filled with the taste of him. "I love you." She whispered against his muscled torso. As he made love to her, orgasm after orgasms slammed into her so hard that she screamed aloud and thought she would die from too much pleasure. He plunged deeper and deeper inside her with her clinging to him. She screams in ecstasy, and both exploded in unison, and lay spent in each other's arms.

He rolled onto his side and brushed a kiss across her lips, but he saw tears filling her eyes.

"Darling, what's up?" He said disturbed.

"I am so happy. I am so deliriously happy because I have you. Delirious happiness cannot be born for long."

"Do not fear anything love, we will live together for the rest of our lives."

"Before I met you, my life was a desert parched and empty. Thank you for loving me through all my scars and wounds. You looked beyond yourself and healed my hurting soul. I am eternally grateful."

"Hey sweetie, we will live a happy long life together." He pressed a feather-light kiss against her eyelids, the tip of her nose, her cheekbones reassuring her.

"You enriched my life with love and happiness. You revived my dormant desires. I am being revived. I feel whole again." Now her tears spilled from her eyes and ran down her cheeks.

"Why all these tears for?" He said kissing her tears away.

"I have a lot to be thankful for. I have you. You are the love of my life. You are the hope I cling to. You are my everything. I don't want this happiness to go away."

"It will never go away I promise." He held her body against his, wishing he could take her fear away.

"In your arms, I knew what true happiness is. Happiness is not how much we have, but the value of every moment I spend with you - to love you and be loved by you. I love you to the point of pain. I feel like have been born again. Thank you for all the kindness you showered upon me."

"Now you talk like a wise man and not like a woman in love." He said laughing lightly.

"I have fears of the unknown. I am afraid you will stop loving me."

"I promise to love you, cherish you, and be faithful to you. I promise to protect you and give you the life you deserve. I promise you this for all the days of my life."

Tears welled in her eyes at his words. He gathered her in his arms and they slept in each other's arms until the morning light.

In the next day, a fancy limousine came to take them both to the luxurious headquarters of Hashem's holding company. Angela examined Hashem's office with wonder. Her gaze roamed over the office, and she found herself staring at the extensive wood panelling, wood ceiling, wood floor, rich rug, large wood desk and over-sized leather armchair. Deep toned and highly graphic wallpaper surrounded the desk. Sculptural console lamps and a mirror added just the right amount of decoration. The office door opens to a spacious room of Hashem secretaries. Hashem is surrounded by more beautiful, well-groomed secretaries than Angela had ever seen in her life. He must have been sleeping around with the world's most beautiful women, she surmised. When he had a meeting, only the most beautiful secretaries were allowed to greet the guests or serve coffee. It seems he knew how to work their characteristics to his favour. He knew how to exploit the skills of everyone who worked for him. She noticed that anyone could just walk into his office. There were no bodyguards. He was totally approachable and accessible.

Hashem sat at his desk and glanced down at his watch in anticipation for an upcoming meeting that was due after a few minutes. Angela sat opposite him watching how busy he was. Two beautiful secretaries entered the office and laid before him some papers. He ran his eyes over the papers rather quickly and nodded his head in approval. The two secretaries left the room and he glanced at Angela smiling.

"You are surrounded by stunning women. You have taken to decorating your office with beautiful women. The secretaries look like models." She said in a jealous tone.

"I like to surround myself with beautiful things and beautiful faces. I like luxury in everything." He said in a matter of fact way.

She stared at this Arab tycoon, and a sharp pang of jealousy and a feeling of bitter resentment and dissatisfaction upset her beyond measure.

"You're not upset?" he asked warily.

She didn't reply but her face was contorted with indignation, and intense pain showed in her eyes.

In a few minutes, I am to convene a summit of billionaires that would lead to philanthropic efforts to solve problems globally, including health initiatives that could save lives without much funding. I will be happy if you attend the summit with me. It will be a good opportunity to introduce you to my friends." He said rising from his seat and taking her hand in his and pulled her along with him to the meeting room.

Hashem's spacious meeting room hosted 50 richest people of the world. Their estimated net worth was 1.2 trillion as much as that of the 3.5 billion poorest combined.

Hashem greeted his guests, and introduced Angela to them, "Angela Collins my wife." He said pointing at Angela smiling.

They smiled and raised their glasses up giving a shout of congratulations.

Baroness Adelle von Vetsera was present among the guests. She was a tall slim brown-haired woman dressed in red, glamorously looking, with diamond studded bracelets she wore over her high red gloves screamed obscene wealth. Baroness Adelle was of Austrian descent, her great grandfather was Baron Albin von Vetsera, a diplomat in foreign service at the Austrian court. Albin was made a Baron in 1855 by the emperor Franz Joseph. His wife, Adonia Doukas was a member of a Greek family of reputed millionaires from Corfu island, then part of the Ottoman Empire, considered at the time the richest individuals of the empire.

Upon the death of her father, Adelle inherited a 75% stake in the business founded by her father, who made his billions from a duty-free shopping empire, and logistics and transportation companies.

"You naughty boy, you marry without inviting me to your wedding! Not being invited to the wedding of someone I once called my most intimate friend hurts more than just a little." She shot at Hashem in a coquettish tone.

"I am sorry baroness, we married in haste. It was our choice to make the wedding intimate. I hope you understand that it is nothing personal, and respect our wishes to keep our sacred event small."

"Small! You invited 300 persons from around the world. Congratulations on your wedding anyway." She said reprimanding him.

"No offense I hope, baroness."

She shot him a piercing glance and said, "Great haste makes great waste. Married in haste, we repent at leisure."

Angela fumed in silence, wishing she could turn her finger into a knife, and pierce the baroness eyes with it. Hashem must have had an intimate relationship with her in the past, she thought.

Hashem convened with the world's wealthiest people and discussed with them how to encourage the wealthy people of the world to contribute their wealth to philanthropic causes. Hashem urged the business leaders to put their money and skills to use in the service of those still living in dire poverty, and to ensure that humanity is served by wealth and not ruled by it.

Hashem ended the meeting by saying, "When you're sitting on billions, even millions, you can easily afford to give generously to charity and not just for the tax breaks."

The meeting ended, and Angela and Hashem returned to his office where the deputy of the Nigerian ministry of defence was waiting for him.

Hashem introduced Angela to him, and the man bowed with respect. The man looked at Angela with suspicion, but Hashem reassured him that he could talk with confidence before her. The Deputy of the Nigerian Ministry of Defence commenced the conversation.

Deputy of Ministry of Defence: "I am here to convey the thanks of our president for your efforts in helping our government resist Boko Haram terrorist groups. The military support you offered to our government last year is highly appreciated."

Hashem: "Thank you. Please carry my thanks to the president."

Deputy of Ministry of Defence: "Our government has failed to tackle Boko Haram in its six-year insurgency. Last week, Boko Haram pledged allegiance to ISIS - killing thousands of people and capturing towns across the north-eastern states of Adamawa, Borno and Yobe.
Hashem: "Sorry to hear that."

Deputy of Ministry of Defence: "We have decided to fight Boko Haram insurgency through various ways; the Nigerian army, recruiting herdsmen to confront Boko Haram militia, and your military support."

The Deputy of Ministry of Defence ceased talking for a while then continued, "Under your auspices and guidance, and military experience, your military support would help ease the task of our military."

Hashem: "My private militia is ready for action any time the Nigerian government need it."

The Deputy of the Ministry of defence gazed at Angela and said, "I have seen many wars and seen many acts of courage but I have never known anyone to compare with your husband. Do you know Mrs Abbadi that your husband is a great warrior? He took huge risks to save hundreds of lives. He made acts of extreme valour during our war with Boko Haram last year. He never talks about himself, he lets his actions speak for him."

Angela stared at the man in bewilderment.

The Deputy of the Ministry of defence left his seat and shook hands with Hashem saying: "Okay then. We will be in touch. We will contact you if we need any urgent military assistance." He then gazed at Angela and said, "It has been a pleasure meeting you Mrs Abbadi." He bowed in salutation and left the room.

Hashem drove Angela to his mansion. The mansion is bordered with acres of beautifully manicured gardens tended by experts. Indoor and outdoor beauty, luxury, opulence, and order surrounded Hashem from every direction.

It was dinner time, Hashem and Angela sat having dinner in the grand dining room. The huge mahogany table took up most of the vast space the room offered. Two tall, silver candelabras commanded attention from the centre of the table, holding smooth white candles whose wax never dripped. Asian servants supervised by a British young woman served superb dinner. The dinner was smoky maple-mustard roasted salmon. The salmon was topped with a smoky maple-mustard sauce. The meal was served with roasted green beans and whole-wheat couscous tossed with pecans and chives. They conversed while eating.

Angela: "You are living in a harem surrounded by dozens of beautiful women. You behave to women as if you loved them. You are recruiting them to cater to your every sexual whim."

Hashem: "This has been my life Angela and will ever be. From birth, I was surrounded with luxury. People focused on catering to every little detail of my life served me. There are maids and butlers waiting on me in a variety of mansions. I had the finest education in the most exclusive schools. I enjoyed horseback riding, skiing, sailing, hunting and touring. I am a man of the world. I have business everywhere."

Angela: "And what about this Nairobi thing? The man said that you are a fantastic warrior, and that you have your own militia.

Hashem: "I love justice and its establishment on earth. In the Qur'an, Allah is described as "the Most Just" Who maintains His creation in justice. Allah wants us also to be just in our behaviour. Allah loves those who are just and hates the wrongdoers."

Angela: "What is injustice in your opinion?"

Hashem: "Injustice is deviation from justice and violation of the truth. injustice is to be unjust towards other people. Blame is only open against those who do wrong to the people, and are insolent in the earth wrongfully. The recompense of evil is evil the like of it."

Angela: "This is why you are helping the vanquished in Nairobi?"

Hashem: "Yes, by helping them I am implementing the divine justice."

Angela: "And you kill for that purpose?"

Hashem: "Yes, if I have to."

Angela: "Hashem, Have I married a terrorist?" She said worriedly.

Hashem: "No darling, you have married a dove of peace, an olive branch." He laughed aloud.

Angela: "Do you have feelings for me?"

Hashem: "I love you."

Angela: "How that could be and you are surrounded by all these beautiful women? You must have had intimate relationship with them. Can you honestly say that you prefer me, over any other women you've been with?"

Hashem: "We didn't know each other, but fate brought us together, and here we are. Forget about my past. You are committed to me and I am faithful to you."

Angela: "I haven't been in a relation until I met you. I have truly fallen in love with you after I never thought that would be possible. You awakened my dormant desires and let them flow to fill my life with joy. You showed me what true love could do. You will always have a special place in my heart. Tell me you will love me forever and you will not let me go."

Hashem: "I promise that I will love you as long as I live."

Hashem then surprised her when he said: "I have bought a grand villa in Florida for you and me to live in."

Angela: "Why all these unnecessary costs, we can live with my mother?"

Hashem: Live with your mother! Are you crazy? Her fatness consumes every empty space. There is no space for us there."

Angela: "Hashem please, speak of my mother with some respect."

Hashem laughing: "Your mother's ass is so fat, if I slap it in Christmas, it will not stop shaking till New Year's Eve."

"Close your mouth. Crap is coming out of it." She said laughing vigorously.

"Now what?" She said still laughing.

He rose from his chair and stretched his hand to her. "Let's make love."

"Now you are talking." She said taking his hand and both headed to the bedroom.

CHAPTER 10

Because Hashem's commercial enterprises were spread over several countries, he used to spend months every year abroad to manage his numerous business activities. When he married Angela however, he had to spend time with her in Florida. He bought her a $15 million breath-taking home. The price is justified by the home's palatial look of its exterior or its interior spaces. Once inside, the guests are greeted by a grand foyer that features a soaring ceiling as well as antique-looking armchairs, chandeliers and a central staircase that leads the way to the upper levels. The residence included three bedrooms, and three bathrooms. There was also a formal dining area for twelve people, a home theatre, and a fully equipped kitchen. The Villa's garden was amazingly beautiful and contained a wealth of the most beautiful flowers imaginable.

After one year of marriage, Angela gave birth to a girl, they called Aisha. Seventeen months later, Angela gave birth to a boy, they called Amr.

Aisha was the innermost depths of Hashem's soul and the apple of his eye. She was the love of his life. She was like a balsam upon his heart. He showered her with unconditional love. He moved heaven and earth to care for her.

Hashem was always there for Aisha. He was there with arms ready to catch her when she took her first steps or stumbled. He was there to make her cheese sandwiches, and tie her shoes. He was there to hug her and kiss her on her first days of school. But most of all, he was always there to love her. And she was always there to love him back.

Hashem shared with Angela in caring for his children. From day one, he shared in changing diapers, giving baths, putting the babies to sleep and calming their cries.

Once Aisha started toddling around, Hashem got down on the floor and played with her. He was consistently present in her life, being alert and sensitive to her feelings. He took time to listen to her thoughts and took an active interest in her hobbies. He believed that his direct involvement and encouragement would help diminish any sense of insecurity Aisha might feel, and increase her confidence in her own abilities.

Aisha filled Angela's heart with unending love. To her she was the hope and promise of the future. From the moment she was born, Aisha was the precious darling of her mother, and they became best friends. Aisha was so affectionate and loving, so lovely and caring. Angela's love for her daughter knew no bounds. Aisha's smile or the touch of her hand could calm the most devastating troubles of Angela.

Angela lit up anytime her son and daughter were around. Her world revolved around them. She doted on them and was very much involved in their upbringing.

Angela would sit in the sofa and put Aisha's head on her legs and tells her sweet stories. When Aisha went to bed, Angela sits down beside her with a book and read her a story.

Hashem raised up his son like a man, a man strong and wise enough to be his heir. He bought him building blocks because that was what he loved. Men do not make good choices in life by accident–they need practice. Hashem gave Amr choices by picking two options and let Amr decide on one that is good for him. The more practice he got making good decisions under Hashem's watchful eye, the easier it was for Amr to make the right choice when Hashem was not around.

Given how important financial skills are to navigating life, Hashem taught Amr to save money. When Amr reached five years of age, Hashem taught him that if he really wants something, he should wait and save to buy it. When Amr saved money, Hashem rewarded him with small toys or special outings.

Hashem helped Amr grow into a caring, confident, responsible boy. He shared with him playful wrestling and roughhousing to teach him to control his physical impulses and regulate his emotions.

At the age of nine, Hashem taught Amr to ride horses in order to improve coordination, motor function and mental and physical health. Horse riding taught Amr at this early age the responsibility of caring for animals.

When Hashem walked his daughter first time to school, and seeing her walking into a classroom for the first time, he shed tears. Aisha kissed him affectionately to calm him down. "Do not cry papa. It is a matter of hours and then you will see me again." She said reassuring her father. She then said to Amr, her brother, "Guess what! Today I'm going to school and I'm so excited."

Aisha was good at school and was loved by her colleagues. She brought home a folder in which each student in her class had drawn a picture of her and written something nice about her. Hashem was amazed, by the time he finished reading, there were tears in his eyes.

When Aisha grew into a beautiful 12 years – old girl, she worked hard to feel grown up and independent. She was busy discovering herself and her place in the world. Hashem accepted this new situation and adjusted his parenting style to connect and listen more. He stayed close to her. Hugged her hello every morning, and hugged her goodbye when she left for school. Just before bedtime, he used to lay down next to her to discuss her day and having few minutes of quiet connection. When she over-dramatizes he offered empathy.

Aisha liked to dance. Hashem nurtured her passions. He danced with her to the music she loved. He shared with her the ideas of her writings. She loved drawing and created some characters of her own characterized by elegance and a sense of dynamic motion. Hashem encouraged her drawing style.

Aisha was Hashem's world – the light of his life. He was thrilled to see her growing. He always spoke of her with a sparkle in his eyes. He took pride in being her father.

CHAPTER II

The river of life glided along beautifully between Hashem and Angela until Angela made a computer search about Hashem. She wanted to know about his past and any secrets he might have intentionally kept from her. She discovered that Hashem had sexual affairs with women that spanned more than a decade. This matter however, did not seem like a big deal to her because these women were just insignificant ghosts from the distant past. Nevertheless, she felt a pang of jealousy because all these women had robbed her because each had a piece of him. She tried to convince herself that Hashem was good to her, and that all his past relationships happened before her time, but such close relationships he had with other women annoyed her.

What infuriated Angela most was what she read about Hashem's intimate relationship with the baroness. Hashem lived a long-term relationship that resembled a marriage with the baroness. She could not count how many pictures the internet showed them together. More than enough of those pictures were of them wrapped up in each other's arms.

She remembered how the baroness was upset at Hashem when she was not invited to the wedding, and how she snapped at him saying, "You naughty boy, you marry without inviting me to your wedding! Not being invited to the wedding of someone I once called my most intimate friend hurts more than just a little." Angela recalled when the baroness also said, "Great haste makes great waste. Married in haste, we repent at leisure."

Adele, the baroness, was not an ordinary woman. She was tough, strong-willed, and brave. She was a woman in full possession of herself and her powers. The baroness created her own world. Ordinary life does not interest her. She emptied her mind of extraneous thoughts and kept it focused on one thing - the target.

Adele had no room in her life for love. She refused to live with someone who falls short of what she deserves. She has chosen to preserve a spot in her heart, for a real man, someone mature enough to appreciate her self-value.

Then, she met Hashem in a business deal. She saw him gorgeous, sexy, rich and strong. His strength and beauty fascinated her. She knew from their long talks that he liked women in full possession of themselves. He loved strong women who feel deeply and love fiercely - strong women who stop trying if they feel unwanted, and just walk away - women who would realize that they could stay in his heart but not in his life. What he meant was love without commitment, and that she accepted, because she relished independence away from man's power.

But Hashem captured her heart and body and lived with her a life filled to the brim with love and passion. She saw him attractive, confident and charismatic. She coped efficiently with his increased sex drive and was a voluptuous body welcoming generously his sexual desires.

Hence, it was not surprising when she could not fulfil her part of the deal - no commitment - because she fell deeply in love with Hashem. He became her lover, her world, her rock, her foundation of trust and companionship. When he walked away, she was devastated and did not know how to cope with the pain. She felt like her life was over and that she would not be able to live her life fully again.

As one of the industry icons, Hashem occasionally hosts business dinners. Doing business over dinner is a good way to introduce oneself to clients, build relationships and seal deals. Business icons from renowned Industries were invited. All guests were Hashem's acquaintances. Hashem with Angela passed by the tables greeting their guests cordially, asking them to dance and make merry.

As they reached their special table, they found the baroness sitting at their table with a broad smile on her face. The volcano of Angela's black jealousy erupted when she saw that the baroness was among the invited guests. Hashem introduced his wife to the baroness. Angela greeted her with a conservative smile and rumbles in her stomach. With eyes so piercing, the baroness examined Angela with a look so scrutinizing, that Angela felt intense discomfort. Dinner was served. The diners ate and chatted together.

Hashem: "Della and I are launching a new business together. Tonight, we celebrate dinner for a 50-50 joint venture partnership between one of my subsidiaries dealing with energy and Adel's Logistics and Transportation Company - the venture worth $50 million. It is established to provide services in the area of international and domestic truck forwarding, storage and customs services."

Angela was surprised to see Hashem calling the baroness Adele by her nickname Della! He must have been cheating on her with this woman behind her back.

Adele said staring plainly at Hashem's eyes, desiring to embarrass Angela: "We have been separated for years darling, and this stresses me out to no end. I have decided to make our relationship work. Co-partnership actually strengthens romances and businesses."

Angela fumed: "What do you mean by co-partnership strengthens romances?"

Adele: "For five years of my life and Hashem had been the centre of my universe. He was my first love and the last. To me he was the handsomest, most extraordinary man on the planet, but one day he walked out and left me devastated. I want to be near him, even if it were through co-partnership."

Angela: "How could you say all that crap about my husband? Show me some respect."

Adele ignored Angela and shot at Hashem: "I can't say this more bluntly than this. You ow me an explanation Hashem. What did you see in her that made you choose her over me?"

Hashem: "Adele are you taking revenge on me? There is no point in reviving the past."

Adele snapped at him, "You took my life with you. You were my entire world. How dare you choose her over me?" Tears came into her eyes.

Hashem: Adele, please calm down, the past is over and we can't get it back."

"I can't get over loving you. Can't you just understand?"

Hashem: "It's over Adele. I am married now. Forget about the past."

Adele weeping hotly, "My past with you will never die, it walks with me. I am one of the richest women on earth, but I am not rich enough to buy back my past."

Adele bit down on her lower lip and wiped away her tears. She said with a regretting tone: "You made me love you, and then you left me to perish."

Angela suddenly burst in: "And you made me fucking insane."

Adele: "Watch your tongue woman and keep your mouth shut."

Angela frowned at Hashem and said, "That woman talks too much fucking."

Angela then gazed at the baroness and shot at her: "Shut up. Got that cunt."

Hashem was caught off guard: "Angela that's vulgar."

Adele: "Hashem, you married a silly vulgar woman. Where did you find her, on a mud lane in the slums of Florida?"

Adele gazed at Hashem: "I am a woman of wealth and distinction. I am pretty and rich. Why did you choose her instead of me?"

Angela: "Yeah you're pretty ... pretty stupid."

Adele: Watch your tongue asshole. You know where you are, you're in the middle of the jungle baby, you are going to die."

Angela: "Don't fuck with me you deformed rat or I'll fuck you up."

Adele: "Let me make this perfectly clear to you. I will never give up on Hashem. I will always love him. I gave Hashem my heart, and I will get it back even if it were in pieces. Do you get that?"

Angela: I don't get that, I don't speak idiot. Are you always an idiot or just when I am around?"

Adele groaned and held her head in her hands: "O God. This insignificant miserable creature causes me headache. I am tired. I have a brain freeze."

Angela: "You have a brain freeze? But honey doesn't that actually require a brain first?"

Adele could not keep up with Angela's vulgarity, so she focused on Hashem: "I wish I could give you my pain just for one moment so you can understand how much you hurt me."

Angela snapped at the baroness: "Shut up, stupid pathetic worm."

Hashem: "Our past is history to me now Adele. Forget about the past and move your life forward."

Hashem looked at both women and said: "I have had enough of listening to your insolence. I will not tolerate your impudence any further. Stop it both of you."

Angela rose from her chair and put her hand on Hashem's shoulder: "Come on honey lets go home. Let's not waste time with this stupid nasty punk."

Hashem lifted himself from the chair, and addressed the baroness in an angry tone: "You deliberately provoked her. You must have been nuts. She is not an easy prey. She gave you what you deserve. You have stirred my anger Adele."

"I am sorry that I offended you; but remember, you will see much of me because we have a business worth $50 million to run together. We will meet again to put the final touches and celebrate the official opening of the project."

Hashem and Angela strolled to the door leaving the baroness alone sunk in vengeful anger.

Driving back home, Angela sat in the car devastated after the encounter with the baroness. Jealousy triggered her anxiety and her right hand began to shake. Hashem held her hand to stop the shaking. She pulled her hand back rejecting his care. The impudence she saw from the baroness sent her into rage that was discharged on Hashem.

"I thought you a saint but you are not. It's really hard to imagine that you had been with others before me. I get jealous over every girl from your past." She said while trying to calm down the tremor of her hand.

"I had my days Angela, and nothing you could do would ever change that. My past mistakes are not who I am. Who I am is someone who really cares about you."

She opened her purse and brought out a small gold-toned pill box. She flipped it open, took from it a pill of propranolol, and pushed it down her throat.

"You have a crush on her, which makes me feel bad."

"It's you whom I love Angela, and not her. This jealousy consumes you without reason."

"I'm obsessed with your exes."

"Stop being so jealous, please."

They reached home. Angela prepared a light dinner for Hashem. She did not eat with him; but rather took a few gulps of wine to calm down further the shaking of her hand.

"Wine is bad for your health darling. Alcohol is not a viable treatment. You would need to be tippling all the time and might well become alcohol dependent." Hashem said concerned.

"To help reduce the tremor, the doctor said that I can take with propranolol, small amounts of alcohol.

After a warm shower, Hashem and Angela went to bed. He took her in his arms but she tightened up.

"I hate you. You are cheating on me behind my back." She said pushing him away.

"I never did that. I am faithful to you. We made an oath of fidelity. I never broke it."

"You have done something that made me furious. You made love with other women in the past, and especially this baroness of yours. I find it impossible to push these emotions aside." She pushed him away.

"Do not push me away; let yourself melt back into my arms."

"I was a fool. I found out who you were."

She knew what would happen if he took her in his arms. She knew how difficult he was to resist. But she was not going to be won over so easily, not this time.

"Leave me alone. I am not in the mood. I can't get aroused."

"Please come to your senses Angela."

"I cannot get over your past, especially this baroness of yours. If anything, ever comes up about her I get incredibly jealous, even though it was all before you met me."

"I wish you could stop this nonsense Angela."

"Of course, you had great sex life with the baroness. Was your sex with her wild and enjoyable as it is with me?"

"Angela please, don't live in my past. Now I have you instead, I do not have my exes now, nor will I ever again. Not one of them is a threat to you. Only your own jealousy; your own selfishness, is a threat to you, and to our relationship. You should focus only on your future with me."

"I am jealous of the baroness and all the other women you knew before me."

"The other women are jealous of you because you are my first love. I am committed to you, and my actions are backing up my words."

"Are you going to see the baroness again?"

"Yes, we have an important business to run together."

The softness and paleness of her skin sent shivers down his spine. A rolling ball of sexual energy rolled southward through his lower body. He put his hand on her shoulder pulling her against him. He tried to kiss her but she rejected him, giving him her back.

"I've had a hard day and having sex is the last thing on my mind!"

"What do you want me to do, begging sex from you? Do not humiliate me with your rejection."

"Do not touch me. I am exhausted and tired. I am just not in the mood. Back off please."

He pulled her forcibly for a kiss. "Wait!" She cried weakly and tried to pull back from him. But his mouth came down hard on hers. He kissed her with all the passion and longing he had for her. All the resistance she exerted vanished in a second. She kissed him fiercely as he was kissing her. She kissed him with an unbridled urgency, a frenzied impatience to make love to him. She speared her fingers through his hair, and kissed him with all the love she carried for him. With a groan of surrender, she gave herself fully over to him, holding back nothing.

The fires of hell seemed to burn within him. The lust within him was harder than steel. The hunger and need in him roared through his veins fought for urgency. She was so stunned by the fierce flames and the consuming hunger that had engulfed her. Their kisses and caresses were hurried, demanding. She clung to him tightly aching for more. He loved her slow and deep, and she cried out, flying with exquisite ecstasy.

She enjoyed the pure physical pleasure that he gave her with his hands, mouth and his beautiful strong body. He was driving her wild, her body tightened, coiled.

I love you." She whispered in his eyes.

"You are mine." He said in an arrogant tone.

She nestled into his embrace. They lay locked together in bed, breathing heavily, their bodies shook from cold sweat covering their bodies.

She contemplated his strong muscular body. This man has the power to force any woman to abandon her pride, and force her to her knees.

They were quiet for a long time until they propped themselves up against the back of their bed.

"Why you have to be so beautiful, so sexy, and so strong? I want to hide you from women's eyes." Jealousy returned to seize her.

"Angela, please, not again. Let go. Why do you cling to pain? Why hold on to the very thing which keeps you from hope and love?" An angry frown covered his face.

"Fuck it, your body is so damn sexy. Did you have good sex with your exes as you had with me? Was your sex wild and gratifying with the baroness as you had with me?"

"Put aside jealousy and instead learn to forgive and forget and not hold grudges."

"Swear loyalty to me."

"I swear."

"Now listen, I have something important to say to you." He suddenly said with a grimace.

"What?" She said concerned.

You have no control over your anger. Your fowl mouth embarrasses me. Your crude aggressive behaviour sparks my temper."

"Of course, Mr Romeo, you defend her because she is your lover."

"You spew out insolent words right and left. Your words to her were offensive and rude. You really hit the bottom of vulgarity".

"Do not repeat her words. She claimed that you married a vulgar woman and that hurt me a lot."

"You are not pleasant to be around. Your tongue is evil and spreads deadly poison. Control your tongue"

"This makes me feel like you enjoy her company a lot more than you enjoy mine."

"Stop arguing Angela. Don't you ever embarrass me in public again, you hear me."

"I am sorry, I won't do that again, I promise."

"Grossness and vulgarity are natural to you. You lacked any shred of decency when you uttered those bad words."

"Woman is a vulgar animal from whom man has created an excessively beautiful ideal. I read this somewhere." She said smiling. She continued: "See, the tremor has stopped. When you take me in your arms and make love to me, I feel healthy and safe and that nothing can happen to me. In your arms, I know the strength of love and kindness."

"You better also know the strength of thinking before speaking." He said reproaching.

"I will train myself to stop swearing, I promise. But you know something, you are also weird. My flaws attracted you to me, you loved my weakness and sympathised with my downfall; you loved my independence and self-determination. I even think my dirty words excite you."

"No you fool, I married you because I wanted to keep you safe when life gets hard. I wanted to stand by you through everything that life dishes out."

"You married me because you loved me, right?"

"Yes I loved you, and now I love you more because you are the mother of my children."

"O God, You do not know how much I love you. Lie down with me and hold me in your arms."

They laid together, his arms wrapped around her.

"I need you. I cannot live without you. You are my world. Without you my world would crumble, without you I would be lifeless." Her eyes welled up with tears, and the tremor of her hand started to return.

"Hush, hush, calm down." He said gathering her close and settling her head against his chest.

Love swept through her, more intense, as she saw his worry, and concern. She nestled in his embrace feeling whole, unafraid, and ready to face anything.

CHAPTER 12

The official opening of Hashem and the baroness joint project was due after three days. The opening was to be held at the super large lounge of the Fontainebleau Miami Beach Hotel. The baroness was in charge, she was hosting the opening ceremony. She was so excited to see the ceremony successful, after all, Hashem will be there, and at last, she had managed to put herself in the centre of his attention through this project. It is true that the project is huge and worth $50million, but to her, the project is not important per se, the big thing is that Hashem will be there and she will do what she can to get his attention.

The baroness knew Hashem's taste in food, so she gave orders to the hotel cuisine to prepare a recipe that would impress Hashem in particular and of course the rest of their guests.

Pan-fried scallops with cauliflower cream, black shrimp, imperial caviar and winter black truffle oil was the first main course served with a Dieberg pinot noir. The second main was beef tenderloin cooked for 24 hours with charcoal leeks and red wine sauce served with the Cake bread cabernet sauvignon. The last would be Chardonnay wine served during dinner which goes perfectly well with the dessert; chocolate-covered saffron ice cream with passion fruit and orange marmalade.

Angela looked beautiful in a black Tadashi Shogi embroidered lace sheath dress that was simple, yet flattered every aspect of her figure. She wore a breath-taking pair of diamond and ruby drop earrings to complement the beauty of her dress. She looked exquisitely beautiful by every standard known to man.

Hashem wore a stylish suit paired with a crisp white dress shirt and a black tie. He looked simple, yet stunning. All the eyes turned in his direction. He was well known, extremely popular, women eyes were fixed upon him admiring his beauty and vigour.

The baroness looked gorgeous. She was wearing an extremely low cut, skin-tight, red sequined cocktail dress that revealed her beautifully formed large breasts, sculptured figures, and long tapered legs.

The tables were arranged in rows at the edge of the dance floor. On a step-up platform were two tables that overlooked the dance floor, one for the baroness and her acquaintances, and one for Hashem and Angela.

The delicious dinner was served, and the diners ate with a big appetite to the music played by a famous band.

The guests were happily indulging in the delicious food, drinks, fun and laughter. Over the talking and laughing, Hashem cleared his voice and tapped his spoon against his glass for a tingling sound, "Excuse me everyone can I have your attention please." The guests all turned to look at him peeked with curiosity.

Hashem stood up to deliver a short speech: "Ladies and Gentlemen, a very pleasant night to all of you. This is a joyous occasion because tonight we are celebrating the launching of a joint venture between one of my subsidiaries dealing with energy and the baroness logistics and Transportation Company. This $50 million worth venture will provide services in the areas of international and domestic truck forwarding, and storage and customs services. The project that we are celebrating today has required leadership, foresight, careful planning and philanthropy, and thank God, these stages have been already fulfilled.

In closing, I say we have much to do. My challenge to each one of you is to keep pushing forward as the work continues! Thank you!"

The attendees applauded his speech. "Your speech was concise and straight to the point honey." Angela exclaimed. He smiled at her and lifted her hand to his lips and kissed it.

The melodious music commenced and the dance floor was filled with young women and men, almost to overflowing. The musicians played lively tunes with quick tempo. The couples held each other close and occasionally swung away from one another. The music then slowed down and the dancers danced to melodic tango music.

Angela turned her head sharply as she felt a hand on her shoulder. It was the baroness hand. With a broad smile filling her face, and eyes dancing with excitement, the baroness said: "Can I borrow your husband for a dance? This occasion is memorable for us."

Angela suddenly felt like the air stood still around her. The words caught in her throat. She looked at Hashem and noticed that he was extremely embarrassed. The baroness did not wait for Angela to reply; she stretched her hand out to Hashem, "May I have the pleasure of this dance with you?" She said smiling sweetly. Hashem stared at Angela and saw that she was about to explode. In order to separate the two women from each other, he had to accept the baroness invitation with the intention of reprimanding her away from Angela. Angela was shocked to see this quick acceptance from Hashem, and tremor began to threaten her composure.

On the dance floor, they danced to the tango music and the baroness deliberately attached her body to his. She started moving in deliberate slow strokes.

"Stop moving your hips like that or I will leave you here and go back to my table." He whispered angrily."

"Why would you want me to stop? We move well together." She jerked her head back and laughed.

She shot him a challenging look. "I still think about you. I still think about us. I will fight to get you back. We are meant to be together. If two people are meant to be together, they will eventually find their way back into each other's arms, no matter what."

"Stop hallucinating Adele, I am a married man now. I have a wife and two kids."

"I don't give a dam about your wife and kids. You cheated on me and loved her behind my back. You broke my heart then left me without leaving a word. I want my life back."

"Our love was built on no commitment, remember?"

"O no, darling. My pure love for you was our strong commitment. A strong love worth living for, I am willing to die for it."

"Adele, please try to understand I.."

"It's you who must get this straight; love is the only law of life, just as you breathe to live." She said interrupting.

"I am sorry for everything I put you through. Adele, please try to understand, you are ruining my life, let me live in peace."

"I haven't known or loved any man before you. You are my first and only love. I don't love casually. When I love, it is fierce. I love you to death Hashem. I won't give up on you."

She continued: "You left me. I felt left out. The man I loved most abandoned me. I cried and cried but you never gave a shit about my tortured feelings. You just disappeared in the air without leaving a word. You broke my heart as if it were nothing - like I was nothing." Her eyes welled up with tears.

"Do I need to cry in front of you so you can understand how much you hurt me?" She said with now tears running down her face. She took a handkerchief from his suit pocket and wiped away her tears. She returned the handkerchief to his pocket, and said: "please have mercy on a heart that has never stopped loving you."

"Adele, please stop these stupid tears, Angela is watching us."

"If you love her, let her know that our past was real."

"So you are torturing me by taking revenge."

"I will treat you the same way you have treated me so you would understand how much it hurts."

"Why her and not me? What did you see in her that you haven't seen in me? I am more beautiful, I am richer, and I am more powerful. I gave you my best years. Why you settled down with her and not me? Why you chose her over me? I just don't understand." She said reprimanding him.

"Maybe we were not meant for each other."

"Your words are like a dragger piercing my heart. You should have told me you wanted me out of your life before running away to her."

"Loving you is exhausting, and thinking that I have lost you is the most exhausting thing at all. I am drained; take me to my table please." She continued extremely annoyed.

He eased her to the edge of the dance floor, and then led her to her table.

When Hashem returned to his table, he found Angela already standing. "I want to leave now." She said fuming.

"The ceremony has not even started. Relax Angela and sit down please." Hashem said feeling how Angela was extremely upset.

"I will not stay for another minute. Take me to the car now." She said in a loud voice.

"Why leaving early darling, I have a little speech to deliver. Aren't you going to hear it?" The Baroness snapped at Angela from her table.

Angela got mad and began to shake all over. "Shut up cunt." She shot at the baroness. She then turned to Hashem and yelled at him: "Take me to the car now I said."

Hashem embarrassed, had to take Angela and leave. The concierge summoned their car, and within minutes, the Mercedes appeared in the forecourt. Angela slid into the passenger seat, fastened the seat belt, then eased her head against the cushioned rest and closed her eyes.

Hashem could feel the tension in her body, could feel how hard she was fighting to pull herself together. But he was also angry with her. She embarrassed him by leaving so early. She deprived him from listening to the speech of the baroness - a speech that would touch on the system of work in such important venture. She was also very vulgar when she described the baroness by 'cunt'

"It was indecent of you to describe the baroness as 'cunt'. This was highly insulting and demeaning. Isn't that a hell of a thing to say?" He said while driving.

"Of course, Mr. Romeo, you defend her because she was your lover." She said suffocating.

"It is true that I had women in my life, but I loved you and preferred you to all women, I married you, and now you are the mother of my children. This is an ample proof that I am faithful to you."

"I hated seeing you dancing with her. She is too flirty. This woman was your ex-lover for five years; she is trying hard to steal you away from me." She said with bitterness in her voice.

"You embarrass me by the ugly words you utter in every occasion. Your response to the baroness was vulgar. You forget that I am your husband and you ow me some respect."

An uncomfortable silence surrounded them for a while. His silence was worse than his anger. Hashem broke the silence: "I will never do anything behind your back but you must understand that the baroness and I are going to meet quite often because working together is essential to the success of the business."

"You both seem to have it all: Love, business, and freedom to do as you damn well please. So, you want to spend your leisure time with the baroness?" She said unable to stop the jealous barrage as it spewed from her mouth.

"Stop making a scene and take some words of advice. Love is based on trust, honesty and respect. A lack of trust can doom a perfectly good relationship to failure."

"Don't impose her on me. I will tear out her spine when I see her again. You hear me?"

"Yes, darling I hear you; but your jealousy will not change the situation."

"You must stop seeing that woman; she is going to destroy our life."

"It is your insane jealousy that is going to tear us apart unless you change your attitude and trust me."

Alone in their bedroom, he watched Angela taking off her clothes. She looked hot when she was angry and jealous. He felt the urge to rip her clothes off and make mad passionate love to her. He took her in his arms and leaned down to kiss her. "What the fuck do you want?" She said turning her face the other side rejecting his kiss.

"Fuck, again! Can't you just get a little break and hold your tongue."

"Leave me the fuck alone asshole." She said trying to push him away.

"For God's sake hold your tongue for just a second. I am going to fuck that dirty mouth of yours."

"Be careful with your words Mister, filth pours from your mouth." She couldn't hold back her laughter, so she laughed aloud.

"There is an Arabic proverb: 'If you grow close to a group of people, after 40 days you become one of them! I have been close to you for seven years now."' He said laughing too.

He lifted her in his arms, carried her to the bed, his mouth kissing her lips hard, provoking the animal in her. Her pulse raced with excitement. She caught her breath at the power of his invasion. His chest was hard as he crushed her against him, and she wrapped her arms around him. She clung to him and gave herself up to the storm he had raised. He loved her so incredibly hard. She was more than a little hurt from his fierce lovemaking, yet she didn't want this to end. They lay still, joined as one, and she could feel the warmth of his passion deep within her, hear the pounding of his heart over the racing of her own pulse. She felt secured and protected. She felt whole.

Angela disengaged herself from Hashem's embrace and lay back on the bed with a body heavy and limp, her eyelids dragging downwards with fatigue. Hashem's lovemaking was so vigorous it left her drained of energy.

Her thoughts began to whirl. Before she knew Hashem, her mental illness - this hand shaking she was suffering from - caused her a feeling of unease, which was triggered by perceiving herself to be worthless, insecure, unloved or not good enough. Feeling insecure created anxiety over being abandoned and the feeling that every day is uncertain. This kind of inferiority complex resulted in vulgarity and dirty words coupled with arrogance to prove that she was capable of defending herself and push people to their limits. It was a vulgar attitude she encircled herself with in order to protect herself in a man's world she had to live in after she inherited her business from her father. Her vulgar attitude worked out fine, people avoided her foul mouth and respected her successful management in the world of business. The fear of men, which, her father warned her away from, had also, resulted in rejecting men sexually. She didn't feel any sexual desire or attraction towards men, and she accordingly thought herself asexual until Hashem appeared in her life.

Hashem gave her what she longed for; love, security, hope for a better future, and kids. She never thought that one day she would have a real family and kids. Hashem gave her all this without difficulty or struggle.

His love flew from him as a flame mixed with yearning and desire. She drank of him as of life-giving water after a long thirst. He triggered her sexuality in a dramatic way. His love exploded her dormant sexual desires and made her experience the ecstasy of love. He gave her the time to discover herself as a sexual being after long deprivation. She felt as a real woman in his arms, and regained self-assurance after doubt and hesitation. She will never forget the moments when the shivering seizes her and he enfolds her in his arms reassuring her that all would be well.

Love with Hashem goes beyond sex, beyond the merely physical. It was a sense of well-being, of closeness and joy; and above all, it was a sense of security and protection. She feels protected in his arms. In his arms, she feels safe and warm, secure and loved. Yes, she is a very wealthy woman; she knows well how to run her company and manage her business; but feelings of insecurity rob her of present moment happiness. She constantly feels threatened even if her external surroundings impose no danger to her survival.

Hashem, her husband, the man she adores, is not just an ordinary man. He is the wealthiest and the handsomest of all men. Women line up chasing him at any opportunity. When he walks, the eyes of women feast on him. She can see lust in their eyes as he strides past.

Most of her negative thoughts started with what if Hashem would leave her to the baroness - was Hashem going to choose the baroness over her one day? Was she a match for the baroness? The baroness was his ex-lover after all. When Hashem danced with the baroness, her body fitted perfectly with his, as if each had been designed to pattern with the other. Their bodies matched and the baroness deliberately intended that every move and touch was erotic.

The feeling that she was no match for the baroness terrifies her. The baroness is wealthier, stunningly beautiful, and most of all still deeply in love with Hashem. There is also one important point to be considered; Hashem is a man with higher sex drive, that is sometimes uncontrollable; and this makes her wonder if she can always match his erotic desires. This high sex drive is running their relationship. This voracious sexual appetite took him to countless affairs. Having mismatched libidos can drive wedge between couples.

She is flattered that he still finds her attractive after seven years of marriage and wants her so much, but can she keep up with his erotic desires for long? The depressants she takes have bad side effects. They drop sexual desire and can make women less easily aroused. They might also cause loss of menstrual cycle, and vaginal dryness. Can her sex drive always escalate to the point of where he is? If Hashem has a raging sexual appetite, that she can only satisfy for a short time, what are the chances he might cheat on her while he is away? She is sure that there are many women out there who would gladly trade places with her; the baroness is on top of the list.

She rolled onto her side so that she was facing him. "Hashem" she said.

"Yes." He said, turning his face to look at her.

She watched him for a moment, and then said: "You are pleasing to the eye."

He didn't know what to say. She reached across and held him tightly. They lay still in silence. She closed her eyes trying to feel content. But she couldn't. Her senses were tingling again. A distant threat looming in the horizon. Not close yet, but it was there.

CHAPTER 13

Angela went to see her mother. She wanted to discuss with her the fears haunting her. Although her mother had a heavy heart, and a reckless mind, she had the nurturing love of a mother. The wisdom of the years her mother had would certainly relieve Angela's tortured soul.

On the wheel chair, in the living room, the mother was reading the morning papers when Angela arrived. Angela bent down and kissed her mother, then sat down in the chair opposite her.

Mother: "I see worry in your eyes what's up."

Angela: "There is a woman chasing my husband and aren't the least bit afraid to go after him. He had a strong love affair with her in the past, and now she wants him back. She is getting on my nerves. Jealousy is eating me up inside."

Mother: "Tell me about her."

Angela: "She is a well-known figure. She is the baroness Adele von Vetesera. She is of Austrian descent. She is a billionaire who made her billions from a duty-free shopping empire and logistic and transportation companies."

Mother: "Is she beautiful?"

Angela: "Stunningly beautiful. She is about my age. Hashem and her were lovers for a long time. She was utterly disappointed when he left her suddenly and married me without even telling her."

Mother: "So you are jealous of her."

Angela: "You don't have any idea what I had been through. Jealousy is killing me. I can't sleep, I can't eat. My mind is crippled. The tremor of my hand increased and is torturing me again."

Mother: "Try to be as calm as possible. Jealousy has a way of destroying everything in front of it without regards. Why allow yourself to feel this way if you know nothing good can come out of it?"

Angela: "Hashem will not stop seeing her and I don't know what to do. They work together in a huge joint venture, which means they will see each other much often. The old love will be revived and my marriage will be threatened."

Mother: "Stay away of jealousy by not comparing yourself with her. Focus on being the best "you" that you can possibly be!"

Angela: "I am trying hard mother but to no avail. I am hurt and disappointed."

Mother: "Jealousy is about fear of the uncertain future and you are well off and self-sufficient. When you feel jealous, ask yourself, 'What is it that I am really afraid of?' What do I need to make this situation safe for me? What is the worst thing that could happen and how likely is that to happen?"

Angela: "I fear in losing control in my relationship with Hashem, I fear of abandonment, I fear losing sexual desire especially after having seizures."

Mother: "But he loves you darling. He is faithful to you. Trust him. Have confidence in him."

Angela: "I fear being inadequate as a lover, especially with a husband having an unusually high libido. Depressants kill my sexual desire for a while during which the baroness might steal him away. I feel insecure about Hashem's commitment to me."

Mother: "A little jealousy is healthy in a relationship; it is always good that Hashem knows that you are afraid to lose him."

Angela: "Hashem's friendship with her triggers my insecurity. She's ridiculously physically attractive. Much more attractive than I am. She is richer, and most of all had intimate relationship with Hashem that lasted five years."

Mother: "The baroness doesn't hate you. She hates herself because you are a reflection of what she wished to be. Jealousy eats up your beauty. Have more faith in yourself; you got something the other people don't."

Angela: "I don't want anyone else to have his heart, kiss his lips, or be in his arms, because that is only my place." She began to sob.

Mother: "Love that is fed by jealousy dies hard. This insane jealousy is going to tear you apart unless you change yourself. Jealousy is just a lack of self-confidence. Believe in yourself baby."

Angela: "Sharing Hashem with her is an awful feeling." Her sobs increased.

Mother: "You are driving the man who loves you right out of your life. Jealousy would drive him away."

Angela: "For heaven's sake mama, you scared me."

Mother: "Learn to trust him. Don't get mad at him just because you are jealous. There is nothing coming up that threatens you; rather, it's all inside of you and your job is to get rid of it in order to feel in harmony again."

Angela stepped forward and knelt before the wheel chair and with her head on her mother's lap cried deeply. The mother stroked her hair tenderly.

Mother: "This man, who so obviously loves you, is not looking for outside thrills. Be kind to yourself. You are just creating your own dream of insecurity. Jealousy is a disease, get well soon child. Get on with your life and stop the pain."

Angela rose to her feet and wiped away her tears. "Mama, thank you for your advice." She said taking few steps away from her mother; but her mother stopped her saying: "By the way Angela, do not forget to put some cash on my credit card."

"Of course, mother." Angela nodded approval while heading to the door.

It was Hashem's birthday and Angela wanted to celebrate it at Tatiana restaurant and nightclub. While getting dressed for the party, they talked about their invited guests.

Angela: "I invited my board of directors and their wives."

Hashem: "I invited a few of my close business friends with their wives. Some of the secretaries of my holding company will be also present."

"Those beautiful women surrounding you and accompanying you to every place you go?"

"They are just secretaries, darling. They have defined jobs and tasks to do. Don't let your imagination get the best of you.

"Have you invited the baroness also?" She inquired with eyes filled with jealousy.

Hashem: "I did not invite her because you hated her."

Angela: "You did well."

Hashem: "She knows my birthday date. She knows my whereabouts. She might come uninvited."

"How awful it would be to attend a party without being invited." She said feeling a lump in her throat.

Hashem: "Trust me darling. Her presence is not important because I am faithful to only you."

He suddenly stared at her while tying his necktie. He said pleading: "I am your husband, you ow me respect. Do not belittle me in front of people. Whatever happened, control your anger and do not talk dirty."

"Do not fear anything darling. I will do whatever you say."

The party began at about nine at night. The guests were dressed in their best clothes. Everyone, wore a happy smile. The birthday cake was brought. It was beautifully decorated with pink and white icing. One big candle sat in the middle of the cake. The guests sang "Happy Birthday" to Hashem after which he blew out the candle and cut the cake. The guests clapped out hands eagerly, and then helped themselves to slices of the delicious cake. The music played and the guests took their spots on the dance floor.

There was a little noise at the entrance; the guests stretched their necks to watch the newcomer. It was the baroness in a stunning black dress showing off her long legs in a super-short mini dress. The entire back of the dress gaped open to reveal her incredibly slender frame. She greeted all the familiar faces with a smile and a wave; then turned her attention to Hashem's table. She walked toward Hashem only to stop a few feet from him.

Adele shot Hashem a coquettish look and said: "Darling, something has gone wrong, you have got the habit of not inviting me to your parties. You have badly changed but I am not."

"Hello Adele, I am sorry. I just forgot to..." Hashem said embarrassed while rising.

"Don't bother darling. I have got you a present." She brought from her purse a red velvet box. She opened it and took a gold chain out.

"Remember darling the chain you loved most - The chain you longed for. I bought it for you. It's 14K white gold Chain Necklace. I am sure you will love it. Happy birthday love."

"Thank you, Adele. That's very kind of you." Hashem said feeling the tempest coming.

The baroness stared at Angela as if she suddenly discovered someone insignificant that sitting at the table.

"Oh, your wife is here too! What a pleasant surprise."

Angela looked up at her fuming.

"Since I was not invited, I am going to sit at your table. I have been single for a while, and I need some company." The baroness seemed not deterred by Angela's presence at all.

Hashem pulled out a chair and pushed the baroness politely into it. This gentle gesture had upset Angela more.

"It is crushing when I hear about your birthday party that many of my friends are invited to while I am not." The baroness said adjusting herself in her seat.

Hashem said embarrassed: "Sorry Adele, It is just that I.."

Angela interrupted: "It is just that you are not invited. I don't remember inviting you."

Baroness: "When it comes to Hashem's birthday parties, I come without invitation. Do not forget that we have celebrated his birthday parties together for five years."

Angela: "Baroness, you are invading my privacy."

Baroness: "Don't take it personal darling. I am very sorry that I have offended you."

Angela said irritated: "I am shocked at this invasion of my privacy. I cannot forgive this cold prying."

Baroness: "You know Angela; I have made some inquiries about you. We have many things in common, Jealousy and possessiveness."

"If love is only the will to possess, it is not love." Hashem said trying to get the baroness back to her senses.

The baroness gave Hashem a long hard look then said bluntly: "I still wonder, why you left me for her."

Angela: "This woman is chasing you in my presence. She does not even acknowledge that I am your wife. I am done with this shit."

Hashem: "Adele you have exceeded the limits. You are ruining my life by taking revenge."

Angela: "Baroness, I would like to tell you how I feel about you, but there aren't enough swear words."

Hashem: "Angela please, no swear words."

Baroness: "What attracted you in her? She is not pretty as I am. She owns a modest company and I own the world."

"She owns everything, she owns my heart, she is my wife, don't you understand?" Hashem said annoyed.

Baroness: "I am beautiful, and extremely rich. Women are jealous of me because I have something they have not. I have the power to attract any man I desire, have him fall head over heels in love with me."

Hashem: "Stop hating other women whose only crime is that they loved their husbands. Grow up. It' is ugly how you act."

Baroness: "I don't care. I am not sorry. I love you. You're mine. I'll kill any bastard who tries to take you from me."

Hashem: "I am not going to tolerate your behaviour. Shame on you."

Baroness: "You humiliated me when you left me for her. I felt left out and excluded."

Angela: "This slut knows no bounds. She is so obscene that she would make any decent person recoil in disgust."

Hashem: "Angela stop it - no ugly words please."

Angela: "She is getting on my nerves. The sight of such pervert makes me sick."

The Baroness continued as if she did not hear Angela: "Hashem, if you were trying to find a replacement, you'll be sadly disappointed, I can't be replaced. I'm the only woman in the entire world who possesses the right combination of qualities for you."

Angela: "What the fuck are you doing? Fuck you bitch." Angela sneered.

Hashem: "Shut up, Angela, shut up. Don't spew your ugly words."

Angela: "Of course you defend her because she is your lover. Tell me, Hashem, does she fuck you the way you like?"

Hashem: “Oh, God have mercy on me.”

Baroness: “Oh dear, that’s incredibly vulgar. People throw rocks at things that shine.”

Hashem shouted at the two women: “Adele, shut up. You behave in a very provocative way. Angela, you must put an end to your insolence. Nothing but your insolence will return to you.”

Angela: “I don’t give a fuck. Your mistress is a fucking cunt – a whore, the worst kind.”

Baroness: “How dare you insulting me like that. You are bad for my mental health.”

Angela: “Surprised, stupid mother fucker!”

Baroness: “Oh my God. Hashem, is your wife mental?

“Angela: “Shut the fuck up.”

Baroness: “I can be extremely angry when I am pissed off. You piece of trash, I will bring you down.”

Angela: “Go fuck yourself.”

The baroness rose to her feet, stared Hashem in the eyes and said: “you’re mine, and you belong to me. What a mess you can be, how hard you are to handle. You make me weep, you make me scream, you drive me crazy, but you are everything I want. If you want to walk into my life again I will hold my door open for you.”

The baroness nodded at Angela with a triumphant smile, then turned around to find all the guests watching eagerly the quarrel. She waved them goodbye with a hilarious smile, then left the birthday party, happy of her achievement. Her message to Angela had been adequately delivered.

CHAPTER 14

Hashem: "Please Angela relax. Do not allow jealousy to get the better of you. Once it takes hold, there is no knowing where it might stop."

Angela: "This woman is driving me crazy. I am so stressed out. I feel like crap. My hand starts shaking, I should go back to antidepressants." She brought out a small bottle from her purse and swallowed a pill of propranolol.

Hashem: "You are the woman I love. I chose you above all others as my lover and my wife. Isn't that enough proof that I am faithful to you? Trust yourself and trust me. Once trust is gone, you probably won't get it back, and if you do, it will never be the same. You must learn how to face life with all its difficulties."

Angela: "After what I have seen from her tonight, I am not stupid enough to trust you again. I felt your attentions slipping away. "

Hashem: "You had better control yourself because I will be seeing the baroness occasionally. We are business partners and so many major decisions we have to make together." He said with finality.

His words were like bullets striking into her. A lump in her throat had formed, and she could hardly swallow.

When they reached home, Angela took too big gulps of whisky and started to cough. Hashem looked at her disapprovingly.

"Hey, don't make a fuss out of nothing. The doctor said alcohol improves the efficacy of antidepressants." She shot at him.

Hashem: "Each time you get this hand tremor, you drink so much alcohol."

Angela: "It's just a quick shot."

Hashem: "You have been drinking much lately. I can't stand that smell; it is definitely irritating; how can I take you in my arms with such a foul, whisky stench? I can't stand that kind of foul-smelling breath. It makes me feel like throwing up."

Angela: "Since I met that woman and there's that fucking wrenching in my chest. She brings with her your ugly past. But I am here, right here, can't you see that?"

Hashem: "There is no getting away from the past. We cannot change the past. You must be strong enough to go on with your life. Trust our love, it's the best hope we have."

Angela: "She frightens me. She jeopardizes my safety and the safety of my family."

Hashem: "Feeling fear is human, but conquering it will make you feel empowered, courageous, and proud. I am on your side, to support you and to build you up when you are feeling down. I love you."

As if she did not hear him, she opened the liquor cabinet, took up a half-empty bottle of whisky and a glass, she filled the glass with whisky and drank it in one gulp. She then went to the bedroom, and changed her dress into a nightgown and tucked herself inside the bed covers.

"Don't come near me. Don't touch me. I feel like a wreck." She said pointing a warning finger at Hashem.

That night Hashem slept on the couch because he couldn't smell the whisky she had dosed herself with.

When Angela woke up in the morning she found a note placed on the bed stand. It read: "I went to London to discuss business issues with the baroness. I will stay there for three days or so."

Tears burned in her eyes from anger. Why would he go to her and he knew that this, would kill her? She felt concerned as she remembered what she had said to him last night, "Don't come near me, don't touch me, I feel like a wreck." It was the first time that she rejected him. She had seen how he felt rejected, and this might drive him to get to the baroness.

She knew that Hashem gets his needs of love and intimacy through sex. This is the way he would express his love to her. But Hashem's previous love affairs with the baroness triggers her insecurity. In addition to her immense wealth, the baroness is ridiculously physically attractive. Her long relationship with Hashem showed that their personalities are also compatible. This makes her feel like he enjoys the baroness company a lot more than he enjoys company with her.

Although she was extremely jealous of the baroness, she cannot prevent Hashem from seeing her or even any other woman. Hashem is a global business leader. He has business everywhere, and his connections are global. Women of every shape and colour surround him in every place he goes. They are attracted to him for his wealth, beauty, apparent masculinity and sexual vigour. When she married Hashem, she was a virgin with no past; but Hashem had a long past threatening her security. The baroness had robbed her of the man she loved. The baroness is not an easy woman. She is a mass of arrogance, jealousy, and obsessiveness. She is also shameless, and is ardently determined to get Hashem – her husband - back.

The jealousy of Angela however, was toxic and more catastrophic because it usually results into depression and anxiety that are not calmed down except with antidepressants and alcohol. Even these two medications prescribed by her doctor, produce nothing but temporary comforts.

A man with high libido like Hashem does not need a lifeless body unable to respond to his sexual desires. Antidepressants and alcohol are known as libido killers. They cause numbness and loss of sex drive. This would definitely affect her sexual relationship with Hashem.

Angela was ceased by an overwhelming fear that Hashem might abandon her soon for the baroness. Her hand tremor got worse during the three days he spent with the baroness in London. She calmed down the tremor by swallowing pills of propranolol with large gulps of whisky.

Alcohol, however, was prescribed by her doctor as a temporary treatment that could improve her mood and health status in the short term, but its long use usually increases symptoms of depression. The doctor also warned that the combination of antidepressants and alcohol could have harsh medical consequences. It might affect her coordination, judgment and reaction time more than alcohol alone. Some combinations may make her sleepy. This can impair her ability drive or do other tasks that require focus and attention.

The combination of alcohol and antidepressants caused Angela persistent nausea and vomiting. She frequently ran to the sink and vomited. Episodes of nausea and vomiting became frequent.

CHAPTER 15

The baroness called Hashem to say that they will meet at the Peventon Park Hotel. The hotel is a luxurious place in the heart of Cornwall's mining capital of Redruth – England. It was their secret place where they frequently met to enjoy moments of comfort and love.

Showered and refreshed, they met up in the hotel lobby. When the baroness set eye on Hashem, her heart melted. His magnificent appearance was truly a caress to her soul. Although she has known him for long, there was no way she could take her eyes off him. His features are moulded from granite, yet his inner beauty showed on his face; there was softness in the eyes and gentleness in his smile.

She knew what that body was capable of. His lovemaking was truly mind blowing. She remembered how he always excited her. He could so easily take her to an exciting shuddering orgasm that leaves her weak and wrung out. She wanted to lose herself in him as she always did.

When Hashem laid eyes on her, it was not only her entrancing beauty that made such vivid impression on him, but also the very special kind of class and charm that she displayed. He found himself again, drawn so easily to her. Deep within him, he was attuned to her love.

She closed the distance between them and pressed a soft kiss to his lips. She said smiling: "How good it feels to look across the room and see you standing there."

With a tender smile touching his face, he said: You smell like heaven and taste like home. I missed you."

"Let's chat over dinner." She said happily.

She took his arm and walked him to the dining room. The waiter smiled when he recognized them, and led them to their favourite table. They took their seats at the table.

She took a deep breath and slowly let it out. "Do you remember our moments together as I do so vividly?"

Moments of their secret life together burst like stars upon his memory. A charming impression was drawn on his face. "I will never forget." He said feeling her hurt.

"I pray to God to have them again. I always travel here in the hope of finding you." A sad smile covered her face.

His face contorted at her words. "I am sorry Adele for all the hurt I caused you. Sorry. I broke your heart."

"You know what a broken heart is? It's like broken ribs. Mo body can see it, but it hurts every time you breath." Tears spilled down her cheeks. Her tears shocked him.

"Oh darling - one day I will wipe away every tear from your eyes."

"Do you still love me?" She said through her tears.

"I never stopped."

"Why then you married her?"

"It's hard to tell. I don't think you will understand. She was a woman in distress. Her company was in turmoil, entering choppy water. The company failed to generate adequate cash flow to meet expenses. I intended to buy her business with a cheap price. During negotiation, she suddenly left the meeting without a word. I searched for her to find that she had turned her fear into a sad silent dancing."

"Oh! Very strange. Why did she do that?"

"She thought I was part of her distress. I was about to buy her business with a cheap price and throw her out."

"What attracted you in her?"

"When I met her, she was a virgin. She never had sex with anyone before. She even thought she was asexual. When we got closer, all her complexes were resolved. She saw in me a man who could awaken her sexual desires. I was her first love. She also needed my protection."

"Is that what you only loved in her, a virgin and needed protection? You are seriously the weirdest person I've ever met. You also liked the dirty words she spews constantly from her mouth. Her fowl words excited you."

"Adele please, don't jump into silly conclusions."

"End of story, you cheated on me, you had been disloyal to me. I wish I had all of you." Tears flooded her eyes as she spoke the last words.

"She is weak, vulnerable, and suffers from neuro disorder. She is jealous and obsessive, but she is my wife and the mother of my children. She leans on me heavily. I am her pillar of strength. I will not betray her with you Adele. Please try to understand."

"You fell in love with someone you shouldn't have fallen in love with. The hardest thing to do is watch the one you love, love someone else."

"I trust that everything happens for a reason even if we are not wise enough to see it. Marriage after all, is a pre-decided fate destiny."

"You have no idea how I desperately crave to be together. I want all of you, forever, you and me, everyday"

"We might not be together now, but just remember, I sill care."

A waiter appeared to their table. "How about beginning with a starter?" She said seeking his approval. He nodded : "Okay."

"I will order for you." She said smiling.

"Do you still remember my taste in food?" He raised an eyebrow in amazement.

"I know what you like and what you dislike. I know your inner thoughts."

She looked up at the waiter and ordered: "For the gentleman, pot of smooth chicken liver with grape chutney and plenty of toast."

She had made him remember how much she loved him. They were very close. She knew every little bit of thing about him. She loved him thoroughly, completely. To her he was the most important person in the world. He wasn't just a star to her, he was her whole sky. He was so mean to her. A terrible feeling of guilt flooded over him for leaving her for another woman. Tears rushed to his eyes.

She withdrew a perfumed handkerchief from her purse. Leaning forward, she wiped away his tears.

"Let me order for you." He said in a broken voice.

She borrowed his words: "Do you still remember my taste in food."

"Your memory will always stay embedded in my heart."

He gave his order to the waiter: "For the lady here; Cornish crab and smoked salmon with refreshing pink grapefruit, frisée salad and brown crab mayonnaise."

She reached over and took his hand in hers squeezing it tenderly.

"You are the best thing that has ever happened to me. I love you more than you will ever know."

"I love you too." He said without restriction.

They chatted while eating the starter.

"I hate that I still love you even though you broke my heart by getting married before breaking up with me."

"Please forgive me. I will make it up for you. We will see each other quite often. I promise."

He looked so broken to her, but she refused to offer comfort.

"Sorry, but I don't need any part-time people in my life. Can I forgive you for choosing someone else over me even if you still claim to love me?"

"Please don't spoil this precious moment. Moments like this are very rare. The point is that I pity her. She needs my protection. She suffers from anxiety disorder.

"What is anxiety disorder?"

"Fear, apprehension, worry, rejection, the fear of not fitting in."

"She is forcing herself to fit in where she doesn't belong."

"She is my responsibility now. She is the mother of my children."

She looked intently into his eyes. "Don't let her slow you down. Don't let her cripple you."

She noticed the hurt on his face so she changed the subject.

"Even when it seems like I want to kill you, remember that I do love you. My moments with you were unforgettable. I still remember the feeling I felt when we first kissed. You took my heart with just one kiss."

"I must say that every moment I spent with you was heavenly. Life has gone without you but never will be the same."

"Though you don't need me now I will stay in your heart. And when things fall apart I will always be around for you."

They moved to dinner. "Order something, we both like." She said smiling.

He pointed at the waiter who came to their table. He ordered: "Chateaubriand for two with chunky chips and fried dug eggs." She laughed: "You are the reason why I love you."

CHAPTER 16

As he entered the house, Angela shot at him furiously, anger smouldering from every pore. "So you have finally arrived." Her brown eyes blazed at him.

"I am sorry. I was held up. It really couldn't be helped."

"What were you doing with her during these three days – fucking her of course?"

"No Angela. I don't fuck women behind your back. We discussed some unresolved business issues over dinner."

"Dinner! You had dinner with her. Fuck you, man! Fuck all this bull-ass shit. Of course, you both conspired against me. What did she tell you – to remove me from your life?"

"Nothing of that happened. Relax Angela. You look pale and exhausted."

Aisha came in. "Dad, mom swallowed pills and drank plenty of whisky.

She was trembling from head to toe most of the times. When she walks it is like her feet are not steady."

"Stop the madness Angela. You are hurting our children." He said trying to hold her to make her hand still.

"Get the fuck away from me." She said pushing him away from her.

Aisha bursts into tears. "Dad - What is happening to mama?"

"She will be okay darling. I will take care of her."

Angela suddenly dropped to the floor throwing up. Hashem raced over to her not caring about the vomit lying by her. He reached for her, pressing his knees into her vomit, securely wrapping his arms around her. Angela doubled over again, throwing up in his arms. She needed a bath although all the washing in the world could not cleanse her of this feeling of defilement. Her only regret was that Hashem had seen her in such sordid condition. Hashem Took her to the bathroom, undressed her, bathed her, and cleaned her up, but when he helped her into bed, she slapped his hand away.

Angela woke up in the morning a total wreck. She found Aisha by her side in bed.

"Mama, are you okay?"

"Yes darling I am okay."

"Dad is a good person. He loves you. Why do you treat him so badly?"

"It was just that I was not in the mood yesterday."

"You drink too much, swear too much. You have a short temper. You hurt dad's feelings."

"I don't have a short temper; I just have a quick reaction to bullshit."

"I want you to make amends with daddy."

"There is nothing wrong between me and your daddy."

"Stop being jealous mother. Daddy looks very upset."

"I love your father so much that I am afraid to lose him. There is another woman trying to take him away from me."

"Jealousy will eat away your life with daddy. This insane jealousy is going to tear you apart unless something changes."

"Little jealousy is good for marriage. It means that I really care."

"Trust is what you need mother not jealousy. It is very insulting for daddy to have you always doubting his behaviour. Don't fear losing daddy to someone else because he loves you."

Angela held her daughter to her bosom. "You have always been a magnetic and precocious child. You are ahead of your time. You are seeing my condition too rationally."

"Your fears are ridiculous. Choose to believe. Trust the people you love."

"You are right darling. I will do my best to control my fears and overcome jealousy."

"Now mama, sit with daddy to apologize and explain."

"No darling, not now, please…"

But Aisha ran out of the room to call her daddy. She appeared after a short while holding Hashem's hand. Hashem sat on the edge of the bed and Angela looked down feeling shy unable to face Hashem's eyes.

"I will leave you both to make amends and get things better." Aisha said while leaving the room.

Hashem began to talk: "Jealousy endangers your physical and mental health. It damages the trust supposed to exist between us."

"Could you deny that you are having an affair with the baroness?" She said still unable to look at his eyes.

"I stopped any sexual relationships I had with women since I married you."

"And how about the baroness, do you fuck her?"

"Again Angela, again! Can't you find another word except fuck, fuck, fuck."

"How do you like screw, shag, bang?" She said nervously.

"Your head is stuffed with the superstition that I am betraying you with the baroness. No Angela - I don't make love to the baroness."

"Making love! I hate this term when used for sexual definition. I love the word fucking. It is just fucking sex."

"Angela, please concentrate. Betraying you with another woman is only in your imagination. Imagination cannot run wild if you know your husband, and I am telling you again and again that I am loyal to you."

"I wish I can believe you. The woman is after you. She wants you for herself. Do not forget that you had a long relationship with her in the past."

"Don't judge me by my past, I don't live there anymore. Live in the present and make it beautiful. Our marriage is far too precious to risk."

"I am plagued with anxiety tremors. I became addicted to wine and antidepressants. I am in continuous fear of losing you. Maybe I am crazy, but you must understand that I love you. I would never dream being with anyone but you. You are mine and I am yours. That is how it is going to be, and no one will change that."

"My poor darling," he said, choking.

He took her in his arms and held her tight. She burrowed her face into his neck and cried. She said, her voice muffled and still shaken: "I love you. God, I love you so much!"

"I love you too darling. You know what you need, sun and air and change of scene. How about spending good time at Little Palm Island Resort? The remote natural surroundings are breath taking for opulent, outdoor dining.

"It sounds like a good idea." She said feeling horrible after the double dose she took from alcohol and antidepressants the night before.

Two hours before driving to the resort, Angela became anxious. She feared that she might have a panic attack and lose control, or that she might vomit in the presence of other people. How embarrassing that would be for Hashem. Hashem might be embarrassed at her mood of anger when she displayed it around certain people.

She swallowed two pills of antidepressants, taking a large swig of whisky to ensure that they were washed down. This would make her solid both physically and emotionally. She would feel like she can do anything. The high doses she took from both chemicals would provide her with confidence and comfort.

That night Hashem and Angela dined at little palm island resort. Located three miles offshore and accessible only by boat, the dining room offered superb dinner.

A cute redheaded waitress approached their table. She was twentieth and attractive, with long legs, a winning smile and an air of vulnerability. Hashem smiled at her. She beamed at him. He asked if they could get a menu. "Sure sir, be right back." After a few seconds, the waitress returned with two menus.

"Angela, what do you like to have?" He asked.

"I don't feel like eating." She said trying to sound casual although she let the pain of jealousy hit her in waves.

She noticed his confusion. "Alcohol and Propranolol are appetite suppressant you know." She said justifying her weird attitude.

Hashem began to feel uncomfortable. She said laughing hysterically: "Hey, relax. I doubt that I would actually taste the food anyway. The whisky and propranolol had disintegrated my taste buds."

Hashem became worried, Angela might do something embarrassing.

Are you all ready to order? The waitress asked.

"Roasted Portobello Caps" with a juicy beef steak. Hashem ordered.

"This is served with grilled chicken breasts or juicy steak sir." The waitress added.

"Juicy steak will be fine." He smiled politely at the waitress. The waitress returned his mile, a hint of flirtation in her voice when she replied: "I will make sure you get a large slice then."

When Hashem was done placing his order, the waitress smiled sweetly: "Do you all need something else?"

"Angela are you sure you don't want dinner?" Hashem asked.

"No dinner. just a bottle of whisky."

"Whisky! Enough Whisky Angela, it destroyed your health." He said extremely annoyed.

"It's a kind of medication darling, ha..ha." She laughed mockingly.

She then turned to the waitress and shot at her: "Now beat it asshole. Bring the order fast and don't dawdle around."

The face of the waitress instantly flushed with shock and embarrassment. She left the table to get their orders.

A bar waiter came with the whisky, and Angela began to gulp down a glass of whisky in a hurry. She took a refill and gulped that down too.

"Angela please stop. Don't do this to yourself." Hashem pleaded.

Angela did not respond and poured herself another glass and gulped it in one shot. She was about to pour herself another glass when Hashem stopped her. He held her hand, which held the glass, and forcibly took it from her. Angela freed her hand from his grip.

"Don't you touch me." She screamed. Her voice was loud enough for others to hear. The diners turned their heads to look at them.

"Who the hell are you to ask me not to drink. No one has the right to tell me to stop."

The waitress came with Hashem's food and placed it before him silently but appealingly glancing at him. She lingered a little too long thereafter to see if he were looking at her. He was not.

"What the fuck does a woman have to do to get some fucking service around here, I am dying of thirst." Angela suddenly yelled at the waitress.

She pointed a warning finger at the waitress: "keep a fucking eye on us, you little cunt, and the minute you see an empty bottle, bring us another. Do you hear me? Miserable!

"Madam there is no cause for that kind of language." The waitress said shocked.

"You really should just walk away before I rip on you."

The waitress broad smile disappeared. She tuned back and made her way over to the kitchen frustrated.

A heavy silence descended on the table. Hashem swallowed hard and shook his head sadly. "I am disappointed in you Angela. What is wrong with you? She is trying to be helpful and do her job, and you are being unreasonable. This jealousy will rip our relationship apart."

"I am not a jealous person. I am just a woman who would love punch every woman in the face that gives you a second look."

"She flirts with you right in front of me, forgetting that I'm here right next to you. Why don't you go home with her? It's obvious you want to!"

"I am not enjoying this. You became verbally aggressive and your behaviour is reckless."

"Hashem." She squeezed his arm. "Are you embarrassed to be seen with me?"

Hashem gritted his teeth and forced a smile. "No, I am not embarrassed to be seen with you, but at least show your husband some respect."

She seemed rebellious and angry. It was difficult to discipline her.

"How can I respect you and you are flirting with other women?"

"What women?"

"Are you fucking kidding me?"

'I can't believe you're doing this,' he said. 'Don't speak to me. Just don't say another word." Angela was driving him mad every second. He was unable to resist at all now.

Angela's heart shattered in her chest when Hashem rose from his seat and grabbed her roughly by the arm and pushed her forward towards the entrance. She resisted his hold and tried to pull away, but he carried her in his strong arms immobilizing her. He reached the car and shoved her into it as if he were herding a bunch of sheep. She crawled as far from him as she could. She threw up on herself in the car, and he breathed the worst smell ever.

When they reached home, she was nearly unconscious. He carried her to the bathroom and called Aisha for help. Aisha was terrified to see her mama lying unconscious on the floor.

"What happened to mama papa?" Aisha began to cry.

"She took an overdose of alcohol and drug I suppose. Help me undress her, I must bath her to clean this mess."

They undressed her, and Hashem bathed her in warm water with a little salt and plenty of soap. He washed her thoroughly, lifted her out, dried her, and wrapped her in a clean dry towel. He put her in bed, picked up the phone, and called her doctor. After the doctor knew her condition, he replied: "The ambulance is in its way."

Angela was in a deep coma when she reached the hospital. Angela received medication addressing comas resulting from overdose. The doctor checked Angela's airway to help maintain breathing and circulation. This required placing a tube in the Angela's windpipe through the mouth, and hooking up the Angela to a breathing machine.

Because Angela can't eat or drink on her own, she received nutrients and liquids through a feeding tube so that she doesn't starve or dehydrate. Because Angela can't urinate on her own, she had a rubber tube inserted directly into her bladder to remove the urine.

Angela's coma lasted three days. She woke up confused and slowly responded to what was going on; and here she was submitted to stomach flushing to clean the stomach of poisons.

Side by side stood, Aisha and the nurses, tending Angela. After regaining health, the doctor insisted that Angela gets home health visits two times a week. The visits focused on helping Angela cope and take her medications at the right time, in the right amounts. Aisha played a crucial role with the nurse in taking good care of her mother, and see that her mother health needs are adequately met.

Angela preferred solitude to think about her life with Hashem. She felt she was losing him. He had seen all her flaws and mistakes. He heard the dirtiest words pouring from her mouth. Instead of covering him with love she made him see her in her most sordid condition - dirty, drunk, drowsy and unconscious. Her addiction to wine and antidepressants worked against her femininity. She was now watching the death of her femininity. The shaking of the hand increased and embarrassed her in front of the people. She became addicted to liquor, and showed signs of post-traumatic stress disorder. She became a bad example for her children, especially Aisha.

This time she crossed all limits when she humiliated Hashem in the restaurant. His anger faltered and sorrow filled his face. He did not seem to care about the amazing looks of the diners, which turned torwards them. He mercilessly carried her in his arms, squeezing her bones and shoved her into the car like a piece of dead meat. He was angry with her now. She must watch her words and be careful not to push him into having to reject her.

She was certain that she was losing Hashem. Losing him seemed unbearable. He was the one she loved, the one she would always love.

She wanted sex desperately to reassure herself that she had the power to hold his attention and to prevent him from leaving her for the baroness or for someone else, but they barely have sex mow.

She feared that Hashem might have sex with her tonight. The antidepressants pretty much destroyed her sex drive. She knew that this was the end of their normal sex life. She had a hard time getting wet. Drinking alcohol to excess reduced her sexual sensitivity. She mistakenly believed that alcohol was an aphrodisiac. However, over time too much alcohol put a dampener on her sex drive. Alcohol reduced lubrication and Angela found it harder to have an orgasm. Alcohol made it harder for her brain to connect the dots between her genitals getting touched and her mind feeling aroused. The fear of the future, which might bring a moment fatal, overwhelmed her.

Before going to bed, she gulped down two pills of propranolol and tried to anaesthetise her panic by knocking back whisky. That night, in bed, the smell of whisky combined with propranolol, deterred Hashem from approaching her. He spent the night awake, feeling lonely and isolated.

On the succeeding nights, Hashem tried to make love to her but she was always semi-conscious. Making love to a semi-unconscious body was torture.

"Angela wakes up. You are not responding to my touches. How can I make love to you and you are semi-conscious? You do not feel me, do you? I cannot evoke an orgasm." He said with despair. But Angela was not there, she was already snoring.

He couldn't also stand the stench of alcohol and vomit emanating from her lungs and stomach.

"O Angela please, I can't stand this bad breath. Alcohol and vomit linger on your breath. Use mouthwash, chew gum, take a bath. Have a cup of coffee. Get rid of alcohol breath please."

Because he had high sex drive, Hashem made sex with her, but it was as if he had raped her. In the coming months, they rarely had sex. Most of the time they didn't mention sex, but if Hashem brings it up, she accuses him of being demanding and it ends up in an almighty row. It felt as if they were distant like two strangers living under the same roof.

In the coming months, several conversations continued between them but to no avail.

"I'm sick of trying to talk sense into you. You have had enough to drink."

"Leave me alone."

"No. we need to talk."

"I do not want to talk. Just leave me the hell alone."

"I cannot endure this anymore. Can't you see what you are doing to yourself?"

"Go to hell."

"You just stay here day after day drinking yourself into a stupor. Why are you tormenting me like this?

"I don't need your advice just let me alone and get the fuck out of here."

CHAPTER 17

Hashem was on another business trip that lasted two weeks. When he returned back, Angela greeted him with a hug, but her eyes were fixed on his suitcase. She waited until he was in the bath then ransacked it. She looked through his wallet. Her heart raced as she scrolled through the messages on his phone.

When Hashem emerged from the bathroom and saw her inspecting his things, He turned cold; when she tried to put her arms around him, he shrugged her away.

"O no. I don't deserve this. I am sick of your constant distrust. I had done nothing to merit it. This mistrust increases the wedge between us. Your jealousy is stifling me; changing me from an outgoing person to someone guarded, controlled, imprisoned." He shouted at her.

That night they ate dinner in the dining room. They ate in silence. Hashem did not look at her. Angela was afraid to say the wrong thing. She hoped desperately that he would begin a conversation, but he did not. He rather gave her a stern look. "I am currently being stressed. I need a break. I will take a break for two months."

She felt heat to the roots of her hair. "Why?" She gasped, heart pounding.

"All I want is a little comfort. Am I asking for too much?"

"What is wrong Hashem ?" She swallowed down a lump in her throat.

"I will tell you what's wrong." He roared. "You anger me with your bad temper and vulgarity." I am sick of being hurt. I feel like you will never care."

"I will not look through your wallet or check your phone. I will not ask you where you are going and I will not grill you when you return." She pleaded.

"I am living with you a life of resentment, jealousy and bitterness. You did make my life hell. We have now reached a point where I must say that our life together is impossible."

"How dare you say something like that? You are an unfeeling bastard". She yelled outraged.

"Bastard! Swearing doesn't make your argument valid; it just tells me you have lost your class and control."

"I am falling apart. I need you here with me."

"I hate my life with you. You are nothing but a foul-mouthed woman addicted to alcohol and antidepressants. You are unable to take any decision to improve your health. You let wine control your life and destroy our happiness."

"I love you. I can't live without you." She said weeping.

"You say you love me! In my arms, you smell alcohol and vomit. You disgraced yourself by turning into a drunkard unable to hold yourself together. With you, I have lost my sex drive."

She looked at him terrified. She begged with a broken voice: "Please don't leave me. Life is not worth living without you. When I am tired, you give me the strength to go on. When discouraged, you give me hope. When I am afraid, you are my peace."

"It wasn't going to work Angela. I can't live with you like this. I expect loyalty and respect, qualities that have eluded you. I will get rid of the cage I was held captive in."

"I am leaving tomorrow and that is final."

She sobbed: "You will go to her, right? The thought of you being with her just rips me apart. Please don't go to her."

"Don't compare yourself to her and feel inferior and pitiful. Your jealousy is taking you to pathological extremes that are ruining your life."

"I need protection and reassurance. I need to be taken care of, though the truth of the matter is that my world has just gone to Hell when the baroness appeared in my life."

"Whenever I'm around a woman, you get mad without reason. Now listen carefully to what I am going to say. Amr locks himself in his room and wouldn't come out for days. Aisha says she could hear him crying as if he were scared. He is crying the misery of your condition. I will take Amr with me. I don't want him to see you in your sordid condition." She fumed. "Don't take my son away from me. You hear me."

"Aisha is strongly attached to you. She will take care of you, but Amr will come with me, and that is final."

She got panicky when she saw determination in his eyes. Panic prevented her from replying. She picked up a glass of water and threw it in his face. He wiped the water from his face and reacted coolly: "I feel like I need to end this so-called marriage. Would you like to get a divorce?"

"How dare you bring that up? I don't want a divorce." She burst into a wild hysteric weeping. A panic attack seized her. Her heart pounded hard and she couldn't breathe. She felt like she was dying or going crazy.

Her hand shaking became evident. She left the table and ran to the living room crying. He didn't pursue her. He stayed until he finished his meal.

The living room started spinning and she felt like she was going to throw up. She gripped the arm of the chair until the episode passed, but it left her deeply shaken. She went to the mini bar, poured herself a generous amount of whisky, and drank it all in one gulp.

The whisky she had drunk rushed out of her mouth onto the floor, splashing on her feet and nearly to her knees. She felt ashamed, disable and disgusted with herself. She kept on crying hysterically. Aisha hurried on into the living room to help her mother clean herself.

Hashem stood by the door looking pitifully at his wife. The terrified expression in her eyes wrenched his heart. Her devastation was impossible to ignore, and she needed support. He couldn't wrap his arms around her in a reassuring hug because the room smelled like vomit and whisky. He turned his head away in disgust.

Hashem seeing her in such shameful condition smashed her pride and humiliated her even more. "I will not stay here one minute longer, I am leaving you all." She snapped as she rushed out of the house and ran to her car.

Aisha ran after her mother trying to persuade her not to drive, but Angela was in a terrible condition of numbness, carelessness and stubbornness. Angela got behind the wheel and Aisha rushed into the passenger's seat yelling at her mother not to drive. Angela raced her car down the streets not seeing clearly before her. She drove at high speed when her car rounded a corner too fast and she lost control. She ploughed the car right into a trailer.

Angela was the only survivor in the car. Aisha was already dead before the ambulance arrived. The medic placed a blanket over Aisha's body and the ambulance took her to the base hospital.

At the police station, Angela was too nauseous and drunk to stand. She was found to be almost two times the drink-drive limit when she was arrested and taken away in a police car. She was too distracted in her distress to fully understand what was happening around her. She suddenly screamed, "Where is Aisha? Where is my daughter? Is she okay?" When she received no answer, she remembered that she had seen Aisha's dead body thrown to the ground beside the car and sunk in blood before they covered her with a blanket.

Still in a state of shock, she began screaming out and swinging her arms uncontrollably as if refusing what had happened to her daughter. The death of Aisha had become a killing pain in her breast. She kept screaming until she fell to the ground unconscious. They took her to the hospital to treat her to regain consciousness.

Hashem received a call from the police station informing about the car crash and the death of his daughter. His beloved daughter is in the morgue now, lying somewhere cold and scary and all alone. He went directly to the morgue and obtained an official death certificate for Aisha and registered it according to local laws. With a torn heart, he and his son Amr flew with the coffin to Abu Dhabi where Aisha was buried in the family graves. He left Amr in Abu Dhabi, and flew back to Florida because there was a long-unsettled account between him and his wife.

Angela was brought out of the hospital to court. The judge released her on $500,000 bail prior to trial, on the condition that she does not leave the house. The trial begins after two weeks.

While on bail, Angela had a complete meltdown and was screaming and yelling. She refused to eat and drink. She locked herself in her room most of the time only to come out to take a bottle of whisky from the wine closet, and shout at the servants and physically attack them.

She rested her back against the bed board, poured whisky into a glass and gulped it down. She poured another glass. Her tears rolled easily covering all her face. She gulped down the second glass. She wept silently holding the empty glass to her bosom. She filled the glass again, and drank it all. The room had begun to spin. She welcomed the nausea and hoped that it would distract her and make her forget the death of her beloved Aisha; but it hadn't. The image of her daughter lying dead on the ground seemed even more vivid in her mind.

Suddenly, the he door was wrenched open by inhuman force. Hashem surged inside. Angela was scared to death upon seeing him at the door looking at her violently. He went to the bed, gripped her roughly by the arms and jerked her to her feet. He charged at her: "You worthless wretch. You killed my baby in a drunken driving crash. You have ruined my life forever."

"It was an accident." She said weeping and shaking all over.

"Shut up, you worthless piece of shit. It was not an accident when you hit the trailer. You were drunk; you had twice the legal amount of alcohol in your system. You were distracted and not in control while driving because of the high doses from propranolol." He said, hitting her face hard with the back of his palm.

He spat at her. "My life is ruined, and you are the cause. You killed my baby girl. You stole her future. You broke her dreams."

She screamed in anguish: "Look at me. I am a worthless wretch. I am not a woman I am a worm rotting everything into nothingness."

His hand hit her across the face so hard that her head jerked back and she yelped. "Shut up you piece of shit." He hit her again.

"Beating me is not enough. Finish me off. Put a bullet through my head." She said crying incessantly.

He shook her violently. "Loving you was wrong. I gave you the power to destroy me. I will not wreck my life over your bullshit. I wish that I had never met you. I've cursed the day I met you. "

She said through her sobs: "How could you say that? You have owned my body, mind, and soul. I loved you more than I loved myself. I gave you everything I could give."

"Stop it. I don't love you! Can you not see that I hate you? You destroyed my life."

He grabbed her hair and violently shoved her to the floor. He looked down at her.

"Your life revolves around alcohols and depressants."

"I am very ill. I am suffering of mental illness. Have mercy on me."

"I don't give a fuck. Drop dead."

He snapped at her: "You know what you are going to face; charges of being drunk in public, drunk behind the wheel, disorderly conduct, and killing our daughter. I will leave you to rot in jail."

He slapped her hard on the face and she fell to the ground with blood oozed from her lips and nose. She wept ardently not because of his severe hit, but because she realized that her life with Hashem was being shattered as a broken mirror spread across the floor.

He spat at her: "You killed my daughter, you cut off a piece of my heart, and now you cry like a hypocrite whore."

"There is no use for you anymore - vile bitch. You turned my life into hell. You are disgusting - I hate you." He growled.

"I have loved you more than anything else has."

"Shut up you miserable stupid fuck. I deserve better than being ignored, I deserve better than you. You have turned me into a nervous wreck. You broke me. You do not deserve my love. You do not deserve me. I gave you the best years of my life, and I got in return loathing and humiliation. You haven't given me the respect I deserve. I hate you. I wish you were dead."

He continued his shouting: "What did I see in you I wonder? You are not as beautiful as all the women I knew. What drove me to you, you piece of dirt."

She said through her tears: "A sad dance – maybe."

"Yes – a flight of fancy from a wealthy man who wanted to occupy himself with some trash."

He screamed at her: "Who you think I am, a toy you can play with to satisfy your ego and carnal desire? You know nothing about me. You know who I am? I am one of those who own the world. I run conglomerates; my assets and profits surpass the budgets of many nations altogether. Thousands of employees work for me. I even own an army to fight oppression around the world. Women of every kind throw themselves at my feet, but I chose you over all other women.

"What did I see in you but jealousy, addiction, dirt and vomit? You showered me with vulgarity, indecency, and resentment. You must have known that I am a man not to be controlled by women. You don't own me. No woman would dare control or possess me. I move without barriers or restrictions. What attaches me to women is love, giving and caring, not jealousy or obsession.

"I treated you like a lady, but where were your manners madam? You should have revered your husband and treated him with respect.

"I am leaving you. I took Amr away to preserve him from being contaminated by your bad examples. you killed Aisha, you cut off a piece of my heart, and for that I will never forgive you."

She crawled to his feet and kissed them. She said crying, "Don't leave me please. I need you now more than ever. You are the only man I ever knew, you are the only man I ever loved. You are my rock, the pillar of my existence. You are the sun, the air I breathe. Without you, I am a worthless scum. Without you, life wouldn't be the same."

She stretched her hand up to him: "Please take my hand for I am sinking to a deep bottom with no end."

He slapped her hand. "I am done with you. Drop dead. I don't give a dam."

Then he was gone - gone forever.

CHAPTER 18

Lately, the baroness felt fatigue and weakness. The fatigue was accompanied with losing weight without trying. As the months passed, she also suffered intense sweating during night and excessive bone pain. Worried about the deterioration of her health, she made an appointment with her doctor.

The baroness was diagnosed as having leukaemia and was treated with doxorubicin and cytarabine for six weeks until her health improved a great deal. She concealed her illness from her family and closest friends with perfect skill, and her pride prevented her from admitting that she was a cancer patient.

The baroness received a phone call from Hashem. "Adele, dear. I need to see you urgently. I am at Peventon Park hotel."

"I heard the bad news. I am sorry darling. Are you okay sweetheart?"

Hashem: "I am tired, and desperate." His voice broke into sobs.

"O dear! Don't cry my love. I will be with you very soon."

Adele found Hashem sitting on a flat rock by the pebble beach. She came up close behind him and rested a compassionate hand on his shoulder. He lifted tearful eyes to her. Adel's hart pounded. She sat beside him, took his head to her bosom, and kissed it tenderly. He cried in her arms like a wounded child.

"Don't cry my love. Never cry for the one who don't deserve your tears."

"She has got the devil in her heart. She killed my baby girl."

"Dry your tears, Adele is here. I will help you cope; I will make you smile again."

"I need you. I want to be with you. I miss our time together. Can I have it back please?" He said through his sobs.

She released his head, pulling away just enough to look into his eyes.

"Be true to yourself. You want to get over her. You need someone to make you forget her."

"Maybe; but even though we were miles apart, I still love you. Nothing will change that. If I could be with anyone it would still be you."

"I believe you. I know that you love me."

"You bet I do. You are very special to me. we'd be together forever. I promise you."

"The worst feeling is when someone makes you feel special, then suddenly leaves you hanging."

"I am sorry darling for all the hurt I caused you. I would be lost without you. I will never let you go."

"I am scared to get attached again. I don't want to see you get hurt. You deserve better.

"I am afraid I don't understand. Are you hiding something from me?"

"I am scared because you are everything I think about, everything I need, everything I want. I love you so much." Her eyes brimmed with tears

"Marry me. I don't want to live with you in sin. I am paying the price for the sins I committed in the past."

"You haven't divorced her yet. Have you?"

"She doesn't want a divorce. She wants me in her life. She is dead to me anyway."

"I'm afraid that if you never get divorced, we're never going to get married."

"According to the Islamic law, Muslims are allowed to marry more than one wife."

"Frankly I don't care whether you are married to another woman or not. I want to live with you the rest of my life. You mean the world to me. I miss you so much it hurts." She wrapped her arms around him and kissed his lips.

"Would you accept me as a wife with health problems?" She said dropping her arms back to her side.

"What do you mean?"

"A number of health problems become more prevalent as people get older. I have health problems. Could you love me the way I am?"

He took her in his arms to quiet and comfort her. He whispered in her hair: "I pray that God will keep you in his care, drive away from you all forms of sickness, shower you with blessings, and envelope you in His love."

The newspapers published the news of Hashem and Adele marriage: 'The countess had finally tied the knot with her long-time boyfriend the billionaire tycoon Hashem Al-Abbadi. The couple had been dating for more than five years before El-Abbadi married the business woman Angela Collins. After separation from his wife, El-Abbadi returned to his old love, countess Adele von Vetesera. The ceremony was extremely grand and over 100 of the countess and El-Abbadi near and dear ones attended the ceremony.'

Hashem and Adele took a long honeymoon. Hashem's super yacht explored the seas and anchored on the most wonderful beaches. They immersed themselves in fascinating history, exotic cultures and stunning natural beauty during a one-month journey spanning the world's continent. They enjoyed the most popular dishes from the places they visited, folkloric entertainment and special celebrations. They had the chance to see diverse cultures all wrapped in one sailing.

CHAPTER 19

After Hashem left Angela to the baroness, and after the death of her daughter, she lived an empty life without hope, without dreams, without love. Her condition became worse. She had to shift from short-term depressants to long-term depressants. She used them as sedatives and sleeping pills. After a while, she became tolerant to many depressants, so she increased the dose to achieve the same effect. The over dose however produced depression, chronic fatigue, breathing difficulties, and sleep problems. She stopped counting the pills before she took them. She did stop caring whether she lived or not.

During the bail period, Angela was hit by repeated episodes of panic attacks. When she went to court to hear the sentencing, she was a total wreck. She was sick and numb and in a semi-conscious condition. The judge sentenced her to 5 years in prison, but then reduced the prison sentence to only three years because Angela did not intend to kill her daughter.

To Angela, the loss of Aisha was the loss like no other. In prison, she sat in her cell to grieve the loss of her daughter. She couldn't deal with her daughter's death. The loss of her daughter carried away a portion of her own soul into death. Her grief was a mixture of sadness, anger and guilt. She felt a sense of impending doom and that her world is ending. Fear, panic and worry overtook her. She thought about committing suicide.

The thought of losing Hashem made her extremely anxious. She felt she had lost everything when the only man she loved left her.

She trembled vigorously when she remembered the way he treated her, the way he left her. She fell into a horrendous pain and felt numb to the world. She wished she would die.

Alone in her cell, Angela remembered her days with Aisha. She liked nothing more than to spend hours in the company of her delightful daughter, chatting and laughing, watching her grow day by day into a radiant beautiful girl, and seeing the way she enchanted those around her. One can imagine how distraught Angela was when her beloved daughter disappeared from her life.

The death of Angela's daughter hit her with a massive wave of depression, anxiety and self-hatred, where the feelings were so painful that she would slam her head against the iron bars of her cell to knock herself out.

Hashem's abandoning her was her nightmare. She was devastated by the loss of Hashem. He got sick of her! He had not wanted her. It was that simple - that horrible. This wrenching agony, this numbing grief, this anguish that made it impossible to sleep, to eat, impossible to breathe without hurting, was the kind of pain people could die from.

Angela spent the three years in jail finding no meaning and purpose in life. A deep sense of self-worth encircled her. She whispered to herself sadly: "I will grieve for a lifetime."

Having served three years in prison, Angela was finally released. Her lawyer picked her up from the prison facility and brought her to her home where her mother awaited her arrival. Without any words being said she kissed her mother's head and headed to her room.

Angela was not in a good health at all to resume work in company. It was only at home that she felt truly safe. She did not want to go to the company because she was scared that everyone might think she was crazy. She fell into a sad silence drowning in her own tears.

Angela spent long months in her bedroom completely shutting herself off from the world where she could ache in private. Hashem had surely loved her, cherished her, wanted her, yet she had scared him away with her black jealousy and horrendous anger. That is why he left. That is why he took Amr with him so not to be influenced by her unjustified jealousy and dark anger.

She sat stricken remembering Hashem. She whispered to herself: "It hurts to breathe. It hurts to live. I hate you, yet I do not think I can exist without you. You are the strength and pillar of my life. You have left me, but it does not matter whether you stay or go. I will wait right here, whenever you need me."

She spent the next two years indoors, and never went outside. After two years in complete isolation from the outside world, Angela's mother took her to an anxiety and depression centre where they treated her with cognitive-behavioural therapy, together with anti-depressants. Her hand tremor increased, so different antidepressants were also prescribed. Antidepressants had not made negative thoughts vanish, but they had helped speed them along. Angela had to return to alcohol to reduce symptoms of anxiety, however, alcohol also increased anxiety, irritability and depression. Excessive drinking led to addiction and interfered with the effectiveness of the antidepressants.

The extensive use of alcohol over time, interfered with the brain's communication pathways, and affected the way the brain looks and works. These disruptions changed Angela's mood and behaviour, and made her unable to think clearly and move with coordination.

When the doctor found that Angela's health was dramatically deteriorating, he proposed a surgery through which they would plant electrodes in her thalamus, the spot in the brain involved in the tremors. Angela agreed to go into the surgery. When the spot in the thalamus was hit with the electrode, the tremor completely subsided.

Initially, the implanted electrodes controlled Angela's tremors almost completely, but over the years, her tremors have started to return. Still, they were much less severe. She no longer tried to hide them; they no longer control her life. With such achievement, she slowly regained her health and rarely used antidepressants.

After recovery, the doctor advised her that she must also keep herself busy by doing something useful. This will direct her thoughts and feelings away from worries and anxieties, toward something more positive and constructive. In other words, she must learn how to cope. She must come to terms with anxiety and negative feelings. Sorrow and darkness were things she had to embrace. She must learn how to run a full business on her own while dealing with the grief of losing her daughter and husband. She could not keep agonizing over past hurts; she needed to stay focused on the present and on the business in which she excelled.

As a successful businesswoman, Angela knew that the only thing that would take her out of misery was hard work. The hard work would serve as an emotional safety valve. She chose to continue working in order to occupy herself as a means of coping with the uncertainties and the sense of impending doom.

She will live with her grief. She will heal and she will rebuild herself around the loss she had suffered. She will be whole again. She will turn grief into something positive. She will stand up and begin again. She will employ her grief to work.

It came as quite a shock for Angela's employees to see her sitting at her desk one morning. The employees clustered around her, simmering with excitement, congratulating her arrival after a long absence. She was dressed in black, looking beautiful but rather pale. She looked sad, though she gave them a little smile. "Now back to your work, we have a lot of work to do." She said dismissing them all with a wave of her hand.

Angela then picked up the phone and called her secretary, "Tell department managers to hurry their asses over here after ten minutes."

"Yes madam, right away," The secretary smiled because she realized that Angela had restored her health. Launching obscene language is a part of Angela's vocabulary when is in a buoyant mood.

Angela convened with the department managers and talked about the importance of identifying the needs of society for their products and services and then directly filling those needs. She stressed on the importance of identifying the highest priority actions that will help fulfil those needs.

She instructed them to structure the business as to maximize profits. This could be achieved by reducing redundancies, make sure they are not doing things that are superfluous, and make sure they are doing things most effectively and efficiently.

She stressed on the importance of saving a portion of the profits and build a cushion of liquidity because this would lead to more stability in the business. She urged them to communicate effectively in sales, and advertising and marketing within the clients' values and needs.

She ended the meeting by saying, "Make sure you expand the vision. If you are not expanding the vision, you will plateau the business and you'll plateau the wealth. Put energy into innovation and research. Keep your eyes open for new opportunities and new ways of presenting products or services for those opportunities. Your job is to make the wheel of work to move as fast as possible, because momentum—mass times velocity—is what will generate superior economic results over time."

Angela then looked at the department managers and said: "Now get the fuck out of here I have a lot of work to do."

Some of them were offended, some of them laughed, because they all knew that now Angela was here, and the wheel of work was going to spin fast.

Angela's business was already established in the market but she wanted her company to grow further through increased sales. She kept detailed records, and knew where the business stands financially and what potential challenges she could be facing. Just knowing this gave her time to create strategies to overcome the obstacles that can prevent her from being successful and growing her business. She calculated risk to help her business grow. She looked for ways to improve her business and to make it stand out from the competition.

She made a business plan that helped her to keep track of her goals. Angela needed extra funding to invest more. She achieved that by investing previous profits back into her business, and asking for a large loan from Hashem's holding company. Hashem did not reject her request and gave her the loan without hesitation because He knew that she was flexible and have good planning and organizational skills. He wanted to help her succeed and grow in her business. The relationship between them was very personal and has nothing to do with business.

In order to grow and flourish, Angela had to start by increasing sales to her regular customers. She focused on persuading one-off customers to become repeat customers and finding customers who had stopped buying from her and trying to win them back. By keeping a record of who her customers were and what she sold to them, she worked out who has stopped buying from her, and who might consider buying more.

Angela regularly reviewed her prices and checked them against her competitors. She estimated the likely effect of different price changes on the sales, cash flow and profitability of her business before making any changes. To do this successfully, she studied the cost structure of her business including regular fixed costs, and variable costs, and the value her customers place on her products and services.

She improved her sale performance, reduced the cost of selling and ensured her survival in a competitive market.

Angela attracted new customers by asking her customers to recommend her to their friends and colleagues, and by advertising in local media, and using online marketing.

After three years of hard work, Angela expanded outside her local area by selling her products and services through new sales channels elsewhere in the United States. She worked with different organizations including wholesalers, retailers including online retailers and distributors.

She developed new products and services, a matter that made her sell more to existing customers, and to spread fixed costs like premises or machinery across a range of products. The diversity of the products she offered made her less reliant on certain customers or markets.

Angela always dreamt about branching out into new overseas markets. She exported her products to foreign markets, and in addition to that, she expanded her product range by importing goods from overseas to sell in the United States.

Angela believed in joint venture. She created novel ideas that other companies have the infrastructure and resources to bring them to life more quickly. To put her new ideas into practise, she teamed up with two companies. The first company was the advertising market arm and the second was the product development arm.

After two years of commercial success, she had enough capital to purchase the two companies, and return the loan to Hashem. She called Hashem's chief accountant to persuade him to accept selling his share in her company to her. To her amazement, Hashem's acceptance came so quickly that she understood he does not want to have any relations with her even if it were business. His quick acceptance although she needed it badly, hurt her a lot. She sent him a few words:

"My debt to you, beloved, is one I cannot pay. I remember how my life was before I met you. I never want to go back to that dreary existence again. In your arms, I learned the real meaning of love. A man is not where he lives, but where he loves. Open your heart and take me in. Crawl out from your hiding place and come to me. All I need is the air that I breathe and to love you."

Hashem read the letter. He gazed before him with sadness. She was out of his life now and that was where he wanted her to stay. He wanted to erase her memory. He wanted to forget all about her. He tore the letter into pieces and tossed it into the trash basket.

Because of her outstanding achievement in brand development and marketing in country and abroad, Forbes evaluated Angela Collins as one of the richest women in the US. She had an estimated net worth $1.5 billion and ranks number 90 on the Forbes 400. Her $1.5 billion net worth made her both the youngest and one of the richest female billionaire on the Forbes 400.

The success of Angela in the world of business, was not enough to bring peace to her mind and to her tortured soul. It was impossible for her not to feel guilt over her daughter's death. Day after day, she replayed the horrible events in her mind, torturing herself with thoughts of how she might have avoided the death of her daughter. Filled with grief, and trying to find a safe place to release the pain, she decided to atone for her guilt by helping the poor around the world. She will contribute in alleviating world poverty. She will not just sit and complain from the unjust world, she will act, she will plant a seed, and she will make a difference.

She established a non-profit fund-raising organization she called "Angela Collins Charitable Organization". The organization had a website for fund raising. The organization was dedicated to help people in vulnerable situations.

Angela started the fundraising by donating the organization 5 million dollars. People across the country and from several parts of the world participated in fund raising. Angela was extremely amazed to see that Hashem' holding company had donated her charitable organization 10 million dollars. She knew that Hashem is involved in several charitable works around the globe, especially in Nigeria, and his support for her organization had nothing to do with their personal relationship. All of these efforts resulted in a huge number of people around the globe raising money and ultimately a sum of $30 million worth of funds were collected for devastated people in the developing world.

The funds were carefully allocated to alleviate poverty by providing food, clothing, shelter and other necessities of life. Building schools, hospitals, camps and shelters for the refugees was also a principal goal for the charitable organization.

The project gained media attention, and as the president of the charitable organization, Angela was invited to appear on The Today Show.

Angela addressed the community, "One of the most confounding, facts of charity in America is that the people who can least afford to give are the ones who donate the greatest percentage of their income. I urge wealthy Americans to donate. Campaign for change; Protect life and dignity; empower communities; change a child's life; Save the starving."

As president and founder of Angela Collins organization, Angela has been an inspiration to millions of people around the world. She was appointed as UNICEF's National Ambassador and toured the world to give hope and fight poverty. She saw all the poor boys and girls of the world - they reminded her of the daughter whom she lost.

Since 2013, Angela has been on field missions around the world and met with refugees and internally displaced persons in more than 10 countries.

CHAPTER 20

After the wedding, the baroness tried to conceive a baby for a full three years before she finally got pregnant. Her pregnancy progressed with no complications until the 23rd week of gestation. Thereafter, her health became impaired; she went to see her doctor. The doctor ordered blood test. The laboratory test confirmed a relapse of acute leukaemia.

The importance of treating this disease in pregnancy stems from its life-threatening potential, both to the mother and foetus. The doctor proposed to the baroness the resumption of chemotherapy treatment. The earlier a patient's chemotherapy treatment begins, the better the maternal outcome. The baroness however, refused any kind of chemotherapy treatment. She even refused all pain relief - she was convinced there would have been a risk, even though doctors told her it was probably safe. The doctor warned her that her refusal was a high-risk decision because this could eventually lead to maternal mortality. The baroness had such a powerful sense of duty towards the baby that was growing inside her. She couldn't have chemotherapy because it would harm her baby. The baroness lived with crippling pain in a desperate race against time, hoping she would stay alive long enough for her baby to be born safely. The baroness didn't think of herself for a second. Her response was utterly selfless, inspired by the strength of the maternal bond.

At that time, Hashem was on a business trip to Bahrein. He received a call on his cell phone from the doctor. The doctor told him about the baroness condition. He gave him a brief about her history with leukaemia, and how she recovered after being treated with chemotherapy. The recent laboratory results however, revealed a relapse of acute leukaemia. Being pregnant with a blood cancer poses challenges for the baroness and her unborn baby. The doctor stressed the fact that the baroness refused to submit to chemotherapy, and that would threaten her life and the life of her baby.

Hashem was shocked when to doctor told him this. His heart jolted violently. "Cancer?"

Adele never told him that she had cancer. He remembered her words:

"Would you accept me as a wife with health problems?"

A shudder went through him, so icy he felt the chill all the way to his feet.

"Where is she now? Is she at the hospital?" Hashem asked the doctor.

"She discharged herself from hospital because she was desperate to go home."

When Hashem got home, the baroness was lying calm on the sofa. He walked slowly to the sofa and knelt down on his knees before her. Her face was pale, and there were dark circles under her eyes.

She looked at his eyes glistening with restrained tears. She held out her hand to him' He took her hand and kissed it. When he released her hand, it was wet with tears.

"You knew everything about my health and what I was going through - right?"

"Yes. I knew everything there was to know about your health."

"You are not mad at me; are you?"

Her heart jumped into her throat when he suddenly fell into deep sobs.

She threw her arms around him, and pressed his head against her bosom. "Sorry, I should have told you that I had cancer. Do you still love me?"

"There isn't one person in this world that I want more than I want you. I care a lot about you." He said crying abundant tears.

"You worry too much about me." She smiled as she kissed his tears away.

"When I married you, I wanted a place where I can close the doors to the outside stresses and just breathe. I wanted to live in love and peace with you, but here I am distracted with ten thousand fears of losing you forever." He said kissing her hands wetting them with his tears.

"Why you sacrificed yourself for me. I will not be grateful." He said feeling the deep love he carries for her.

"I gave up my life to save my baby girl; to give you back Aisha the daughter you lost. When I was diagnosed with cancer, my one concern was for the unborn child I was carrying."

"I don't want another Aisha. I want you." He said weeping again.

"I love you enough to fight for you. The sacrifice is meant for you love. My creed is love and you are its only tenet. I love you this much."

"I don't deserve all this love. I am sorry that I hurt you. Please forgive me."

"I forgave you a long time ago. What pleasure it must be to a woman to suffer for the one she loves. Let's live every day as if it were going to be our last."

"Yes my love. By your side, that's all I want to be. I want all of you every day." He held her close to his heart and dissolved into another round of weeping.

At 35 weeks of gestation, the baroness' general health declined. The doctors felt time had run out, and performed an emergency Caesarean. The baroness came from the anaesthetic to hear the news that her daughter had survived the traumatic delivery. Fortunate enough the baby had no cancer transmitted to her from her mother.

After giving birth, the baroness held her healthy new-born baby girl for a few minutes. The baby was then taken to the baby nursery. The baroness wanted her baby close to her but she had to accept keeping a six-month-old baby in the nursery for at least one week.

Six hours after Caesarean, the baroness developed generalized purpura and petechiae, gingival bleeding, and operative wound bleeding. A blood transfusion was given, and the baroness refused to stay further in the hospital and to be transferred to her house where she agreed to undergo chemotherapy.

Two months later, the baroness was growing weaker and was succumbing to the cancer which was spreading through her body. She was getting more tired and weak by the day. Now the cancer was everywhere, but the baroness battled leukaemia for two more years in order to see her daughter growing beautifully before her eyes. Aisha was brought frequently to see her mother in bed. The baroness played with her, hugged her and kissed her and felt that she was a piece of her. She laughed at her innocence and felt proud that she had managed to keep her baby safe against the intoxication with chemotherapy, which intoxicated her body.

The night of the baroness death was long and sad. At that night, the nurse gave her a strong sedative to kill the unbearable pain. The baroness went into a deep sleep for long hours. Hashem stayed by her bed waiting for her to wake up. She woke up drowsy. Hashem lifted her up from the bed. She grasped his neck and pulled herself up to him. He carried her to the living room and sat her on the sofa. He sat beside her and took her in his arms. She rested her head against his chest and listened to the steady strong beat of his heart. She loved the feel of his warm skin and breathed in his familiar scent deeply.

Aisha came with her nursemaid to say goodnight to her mother.

"Mama, are you still sick?" Aisha inquired.

"The illness is gone; the pain has ceased and I love you so much." The baroness said wiping a tear away. The baroness then held Aisha tightly in her arms and kissed her on both cheeks. Aisha kissed her father goodnight and left to her room with the nursemaid.

Hashem kissed her hair tenderly. She turned her face up to him. A brief smile flashed over her tear stained face.

"This dying is boring."

"Don't say that, you are not dying."

"Loving you has been the best thing that has ever happened to me."

"Your love is embedded in my soul. You know that."

"I know that God is punishing me because I am bad. I stole you from her and made you mine."

"I came to you by my own free will. She broke my heart."

"After you married her; I was overwhelmed by an insatiable wish to be with you every moment, nothing and no one else matter what." She laboured to speak every word.

He ran his fingers through her hair, and she looked up at him. He leaned down and kissed her tenderly. She pulled her face away, buried it in his chest. He felt her sobbing.

"Oh Hashem, I love you so much. To lose you is my worst fear."

"Don't fear anything darling, by your side I will always be."

"Yes, it is just you and ne together forever."

"Tell me a story." She said suddenly.

"You are my story. You are my great love."

"A man experienced in women must know a lot about them. How do you see women?" She asked half-asleep in his arms.

He knew that she wanted to hear something that would distract her from the pain clawing at her.

"There is a big similarity between nature and woman. Nature is characterized by climate changes. Women change like nature. When a woman falls in love, she could be a storm, an earthquake, or a breeze.

"The stormy woman is unpredictable, she is a rebel, she contains her man all the time, and she owns everything in him, times and feelings. She leaves without a word leaving her man confused and heartbroken. If she feels that he doesn't belong to her anymore, she turns against him to find himself in the end swept by a violent wind. The stormy woman does not retreat or forgive, she does not believe in seasons, because she is all seasons.

"The earthquake woman is the most dangerous of all women. She is violent; the lightening in her eyes attracts all men. She never calms down. Man in her arms does not know when he would enjoy warmth or when he will be pushed away. She adores man, but she worships herself more. Her journey starts when the earth quakes beneath her feet and ends when the volcano erupts, and in between many victims must fall to feed her ego.

"And then we have you darling; the breeze woman. She is an angel emanating perfume beauty and femininity. She is tender and dreamy. She contains man without uproar and without asking him to surrender. She is able to occupy the land without armies or clamour.

"Her gentleness is her powerful weapon, and her smooth dreams impose on man order and commandment; when she arrives from a long journey, she prefers to rest on the shore because she doesn't like departure.

"She gives man everything he desires without claiming that she knows the keys of his heart. She is the most refined class of women; she is the flowers in trees, and the gentle waves of rivers rolling smoothly upon the shores."

"When I am gone go to her. Go to the stormy woman, she loves you." She said, a sad smile on her face.

A pain knifed her body and she shook convulsively in his arms.

"Oh Hashem! This is no way to live. I am bored with it all. I am going away tonight." She said burying her face in his chest from pain.

"I have faith in you. I know you can get through this. There is always hope." He said consoling her.

"I have long had the taste of death on my tongue. I smell death."

"You are not going to die Adele. You will live long enough to see Aisha's children."

"Sorry darling, but I feel a certain difficulty in continuing to exist. I guess this thing is going to get me."

"Just have faith that everything will work out for the best."

"Living is too hard right now. Dying is easy. Let me die."

His body shivered and the tears ran quicker down his face.

"Do not stand at my grave and weep. I am not there. I did not die. I am embedded in your soul for an eternity." These were her last words.

Suddenly she went limp in his arms and the sound of her breathing ceased. She was light and fragrant. He carried the lifeless body to the bedroom and laid it gently on the bed and wept bitterly. He grieved for her, for his orphan daughter and for himself.

CHAPTER 21

The news of the baroness death spread all over the world. Details of her death spread quickly, overshadowing all other news stories. The news emphasized the fact that the baroness left behind her only daughter - a three-year-old girl that looks just like her daddy.

Angela's eyes filled up with tears as she heard the news. Not attending the funeral is disrespectful, and attending it is a duty towards the man she loved. Angela attended the burial service, which was held in the Church of England - UK.

Instead of limousines, there were chariots pulled by black horses and at the church, there were more flowers than a high society wedding.

Angela sat in the church at the front. The prayers were offered, then the casket was brought out of the funeral home and pallbearers carried it on their shoulders. The coffin was put in an open chariot, and the chariot was driven off to the cemetery. The coffin was followed by other chariots. The casket was lowered into the ground, and the flowers were thrown onto the casket. After covering up the grave, Hashem with Aisha standing beside him, received condolences from the family and close acquaintances.

Angela was the last to stay. Grief tore at her insides like a tornado, as she approached Hashem and the little girl. When she saw his eyes wetted with tears, she could not hold her tears and let them out. She was not crying over the baroness but for the agony Hashem was going through. His tears reminded her of the tears he shed over their daughter, Aisha.

"My name is Angela." She told the little girl. She knelt down. "And what's your name?"

"Aisha." Said the little girl.

Tears streamed down Angela's eyes. She gave Aisha a long hug and a kiss on the cheek. She rose to her feet with tears in her eyes. She stared at Hashem. His eyes glistened with unshed tears.

"I am sorry to hear about your loss. Please accept my deepest condolences. I am here for you if you need anything." She said feeling the quickening beat of her heart.

Her broken voice reminded him with his days with her. His stubborn tears fell down his cheeks and wrenched at her heart.

"She loved me. She loved me as no woman ever loved man before. She sacrificed herself to give me another Aisha, and that hurts so much." He said with a broken voice.

"Let your tears come. Let them water your soul. Sometimes a good cry is just what you need to release all the hurt you have built up inside." She said with tears overflowing.

She stared at the sad little girl with a tormented heart. A terrible shaking seized her. She began to shiver like a leaf in a violent wind.

"O God, you are shaking!" He said concerned.

"You know how to calm me down."

"How", he said as if he had forgotten.

"May I borrow your embrace for a second?" He shrugged his shoulders in a way she could tell he was saying yes.

She held him dearly for long moments hoping the tremor would subside.

"Do not forget that I loved you too, and I am still am. I love you more than you will ever know. I miss you so much it hurts, and the worst part is you do not care." She kissed his left cheek then buried her face in the juncture of his neck and shoulder.

"O God, I am a worthless piece of trash without you. When you left, I lost a part of me. Hug the hurt. Kiss the broken. Love the lonely." She said weeping and shaking uncontrollably in his arms.

"You hurt me a lot. I will never get close enough for you to hurt me again."

She disengaged herself and looked into his eyes: "Time heals all wounds." She said wiping away his tears with her fingers and patting his cheek tenderly.

"I am sick and tired. I want to feel like me again." He said with a deep sigh.

"Then go to the heart that never stopped loving you. I will move heaven and earth to make you happy." A sad smile covered her face.

She leaned forward and brushed a feathery kiss across his lips.

"Miss me a little – but not too long." She said heading back to the car.

"Can I walk you to the car?" He said noticing her unsteady walk. She pointed at a nurse in the car who came quickly to support her. Angela leaned on her while walking to the car.

"Angela, don't you want a divorce?" He said suddenly as if he remembered something she might need in her present circumstances.

Her heartbeat fast, she turned around to face him. "No." A deep sadness radiated plainly in her voice.

"Why not?" He asked looking straight into her eyes.

"A wish of a woman who longs to resume her life with the only man she has ever loved."

"You came all the way from Florida even though you were sick?"

"I just wanted you to know how much I care. I will be always there for you."

She continued heading to the car, but she suddenly stopped as if she remembered something that would keep the sad mood away from him. "I am also here to show you what a fucking awesome woman you lost." She said with a naughty smile.

"You did not forget to bring your fowl mouth with you." He smiled, and then laughed lightly.

"Don't you ever forget that I was the one who loved you even when you gave me a thousand of reasons not to" He said recalling his happy moments with her.

"Life is only beautiful when I am with you. You are still what matters most to me, and I am never going to give that up."

The car drove away, and Hashem kept watching it until it disappeared. He couldn't help the sadness he felt when he'd seen her, sick, vulnerable, defeated, and alone. His resentment towards her was slowly receding as his caring for her deepened.

Two years had rolled away and Hashem did not contact Angela. She felt empty, neglected and very much alone; but her hope did not wane that one day he will join her.

She murmured to herself: "Strong women would rather be alone than waste time with assholes."

CHAPTER 22

The war between Boko Haram and the Nigerian government has killed 20,000 people in six years and driven 2.3 million people from their homes. Quite recently, 86 people, including children, were killed in a series of attacks on a village in northern Nigeria. The Boko Haram fighters firebombed huts and opened fire on civilians in the village of Dalori, leaving bullet-ridden and charred bodies strewn across the streets.

Witnesses said that they heard the screams of children burning to death as huts and homes were razed to the ground. Nigerian troops were initially unable to fight off the attackers, and Boko Haram fighters only retreated after reinforcements arrived with heavier weaponry.

United Nations humanitarian officials urged international donors to ramp up financial support for relief efforts.

On Tuesday, April 15, 2014, the terrorist organization Boko Haram attacked a girls' school in Chibok, Borno state, in northern Nigeria, abducting between 250-300 young school girls. On May 5, Boko Haram took advantage of a distracted military and attacked the unprotected town of Gamboru Ngala, reportedly killing up to 300 civilians.

Since its inception, Boko Haram's primary areas of focus had been in the northern states of Yobe, Kano, Bauchi, Borno and Kaduna.

As part of the sustainable development goals, the United Nations is urging the international community to help end poverty in African countries affected by conflicts and economic instability. One of the tools to end poverty is to provide children with the knowledge and life skills they need to realize their full potential. Training teachers, building new schools and breaking down barriers that prevent many children and girls from attending school, could achieve this.

Since no fewer than 10.5 million Nigerian children are out of school, Angela's charity foundation decided to help alleviate poverty by building a school in Gwoza a local town in Borno State. The aim of the school was to take care of street children. The majority of the children were former street children, some were orphans or had parents who were too sick or too poor to provide for them. The school gave free education for several hundred children who would be otherwise on the streets. The emphasis was on giving the children plenty of food, lots of love and understanding.

Angela decided to visit the school and see how much progress had been done there. After a long trip, the Boeing landed in Maiduguri international airport. Maiduguri is the capital city of Borno State.

Angela visited a classroom. The desks were lined up in neat rows all facing the teacher and the blackboard at the front of the room. Boys and girls sat in pairs at separate desks. Their age ranged from 5-7 years old. Angela sat with the students listening carefully to the teacher. She did not understand the language but she realized the interest of the children in learning when saw the sign of interest drawn on their faces as they listened attentively to the teacher.

After the class, Angela convened with the administration and inquired about student enrolment, teaching experience, and student transportation. Afterwards, the school invited Angela to a lunch, followed by Nigerian coffee.

Angela's visit ended. She was about to leave when she heard shots roaring through the streets. Three more blasts rattled off, and a deadly metal explosive of a grenade clanked on the ground and the school shook with concussion. Angela's stomach flipped as she heard the scream of the children.

Gunmen in pickup trucks attacked the village of Gwoza. They separated men from women, forced the men to kneel down on the ground and shot them with assault rifles and automatic weapons. The women and children were herded together and shipped in trucks to unknown location after burning most of the village with petrol bombs.

The Boko Haram militants entered the school and opened fire on school staff and children, killing ten people, including three children. Amid this panic, the school staff and the children ran frightened in every direction. Angela ran to the school courtyard and managed to hide behind a dumpster. The militants killed the remaining men and crammed the women and children in trucks to an unknown location. The militants then sat the classrooms on fire.

Angela kept motionless in her hiding place for an hour until the militants parted. When she felt reasonably safe, she rose from her hiding place, and stepped cautiously forward. Slipping through the school gate, she ran aimlessly, not knowing where she was going.

Angela was unaware of her surroundings. Shaking by reliving the massacre, she felt that in this place she was just as unsafe. She had no other alternative but to run deeply into the Sumbisa forest. Angela ran fast as she could, tears spilling down her face, the fear of the insurgents that may brutalize her consumed her thoughts. She was determined not to be caught. She ran harder hearing the footsteps of the assailants coming after her. She found a bush and hid under it, and kept still until the sound of the footsteps became distant. She stayed under the bush for hours, all her body trembling with fear.

Trying to get comfortable, she lay for a few minutes on her back, but she heard the wailing of a child. She walked around searching for the direction of the sobs. She found thick herbage. She removed the herbage to find a little girl hiding beneath the herbage crying for the horror of the massacre she had seen at school.

Angela bit back a sob as she pushed herself to her knees. "Hey, my little girl. Do not cry, I am here. I am like your mama."

The little girl reached her arms up to Angela and said "Mama." Angela took her in her arms and kissed her tenderly.

"What's your name darling?" Angela asked with her hand caressing the girl's hair and face.

"Aisha." The girl replied.

When Angela heard the name "Aisha", an enormous pain broke the wall of grief that had built up inside of her for years. The sobs came out of her like a tidal wave wracking her body, tearing her heart. She sobbed uncontrollably holding the little girl tightly in her arms.

Dozens of heavily armed, Boko Haram militants swarmed all around. They spotted Angela and the little girl. Their leader approached Angela and looked cruelly into her eyes. He stretched his hands down ordering her to give him the little girl. Angela's heart thrummed, threatening to burst from her chest at his words. She clutched the little girl to her chest refusing to leave her.

She shouted at him, "She is my daughter. I will not allow you to harm her. You'll have to kill me first."

The leader of the insurgents had no time to argue with her about the girl, because he had more important things to do. The government troops were closing in and were already on his trail. Besides, the white woman could be useful in any bargaining with the federal government.

Angela was taken to a remote area where she was detained with the little girl in a cottage made of mud. Two militants were assigned to watch over her, one stayed with Angela and the little girl, and the other was stationed outside of the cottage. At dawn, Angela could hear muffled sounds of machine guns in the distance along with some rifle fire.

A man wearing a military battle dress with a battle rifle hung on his back and with a bayonet held in the grip of his right hand, was moving quickly between the trees like a jaguar ready to pounce. He drew his bayonet and faster than a wraith of hell, came behind the insurgent who was guarding the outside of the cottage, and yanked back his head, and thrust the bayonet fully into his throat and twisted. The assassin was shocked by the lightning fast assault, his eyes opening wide, blood gushed from his throat. The man gurgled, sputtered and died. The assailant withdrew the bayonet, wiped it on the dead man's shirt and stowed it.

The attacker kicked the door of the cottage open, and in a split second, stabbed his bayonet repeatedly into the militant side. The attacker turned back amazed to be stabbed furiously again in his neck, throat and head. The militant fell to the ground drowned in his blood.

Angela screamed in horror. She has not seen manslaughter before; the spilled blood stained the ground and tarnished her hair and face.

Angela thought it was her turn to be slaughtered, and her grip tightened further on the little girl fearing that the attacker might hurt her. She could not look up at the attacker, she was afraid to see a Boko Haram monster that was going to abuse her without mercy.

She heard a firm voice ordering her, "Now on your feet".

"I can't move." She said through tearful sobs and clinging hard to the little girl.

"Release the girl and get on your feet." He said in a harsh voice.

She said with her whole body shaking with her sobs, "I will not let her go, she is my baby - her name is Aisha."

He swallowed hard. His tensed facial features slackened, the hard glint in his eyes softened. The panic in her voice was heart wrenching. She seemed far more worried about the girl than she had been about herself.

He bent down and tenderly put his arms on her shoulder. "It's all right now. I will not hurt you. I will take care of you."

She could not believe her ears. It is Hashem's voice. She looked up at him in utter amazement. Her whole body started to shake uncontrollably.

"Come, let's get out of here." Hashem said grabbing Angela by the arm and yanking her to her feet.

Angela leaned heavily on Hashem's arm, clutching the baby girl to her chest.

One of Hashem's aids came rushing into the cottage.

"Get the girl out of here." Hashem ordered pointing at the little girl.

Angela yelled, "Don't touch my baby. I will carry her as long as she will let me."

Armed with rifles, machine guns and grenades, Hashem and his militia, moved with Angela, carrying the little girl through the dense jungle of the Sambisa forest heading to the direction of the city of Borno.

After a one-hour walk, they encountered a strong enemy fire coming from well-concealed, defensive positions.

Hashem seated Angela and the girl under a dense canopy of trees where no one can see them. Two men were left behind to guard Angela and the girl.

Hashem urged his militia to march forward in the face of intense fire. He moved to the front of his militia and led a fierce assault on the hostile enemy. With bullets striking all over around him, he fought furiously, encouraging, and inspiring his men to defeat the enemy forces.

Hashem and his men returned to Angela and the girl and all encamped till the morning under the dense canopy of the trees. The morning dawn broke in upon the scene of bloodshed.

At dawn Boko Haram insurgents attacked Hashem and his men again. Hashem repulsed the attacks with sweeping machine gunfire. With the aid of his riflemen, they killed 20 insurgents and wounded another dozen.

Hashem and his troops marched forward in haste, but his troops were ambushed from all sides with battle rifles and guns. Two Hashem's men went down under the initial attack, but he got his boys to cover, directed their fire, and then led a flanking manoeuvre that resulted in the complete destruction of the ambushing forces.

The explosive sound of the gun shots drove Angela to the brink of madness, who was now alternating between constant weeping and worrying for the girl.

Hashem knew that Boko Haram militants were in hot pursuit of his troops, and that waves of other attacks would come back repeatedly.

His militia must then move quickly to a hiding place from which he could launch a sudden attack against the enemy. They found a shallow muddy canal. Everyone crouched low in the canal, weapons held ready.

Hashem's militia were discovered, an insurgent, with bayonet drawn rushed out screaming, "Allah Akbar". His comrades, with bayonets also charged and tried to flank Hashem and his men. Hashem and his men jumped out of the trenches to meet them. The insurgent cut down one of Hashem's men, then another. It was a brutal hand to hand fighting. It lasted about fifteen minutes after which Hashem's men routed the enemy while sustaining minimal casualties.

Hashem and his troops left the canal and marched swiftly towards a safer place, but were encountered with intense automatic weapons and grenade fire. Hashem and three of his men moved forward to neutralize an enemy machine gun position, which was hampering the troops' advance. Despite heavy enemy fire and grenade barrages, Hashem moved to an exposed position ahead of his comrades, assaulted and destroyed the machine gun hiding place, and killing two enemy insurgents.

The insurgents however attacked fiercely and penetrated the lines of Hashem's men. Hashem quickly returned and placed his men in defensive positions to repel the attack. In a daring defence, he personally charged them with carbine, rifle, and grenades, inflicting many casualties. Disregarding the intense enemy fire, he then charged forward firing the machine gun, shouting orders and rallying his men, thus maintaining the momentum of the attack. His dauntless leadership and personal courage so inspired his men that they stormed into the hostile position and used their bayonets with such lethal effect, that the enemy fled in wild disorder.

Hashem militia continued marching to a safe landing site for the helicopter to pick up Angela and the girl to safety. After a long walk, they found a clearing convenient for helicopter landing. Through his C31 communication equipment, Hashem defined his position, and asked the military for a rescue helicopter.

After half an hour, the helicopter appeared in the air then landed safely in the appointed spot. Hashem grabbed Angela's arm and rushed to the rescue helicopter. Suddenly, their ears were exploding with the raucous sound of gunfire. Bullets were raging furiously into the air. The noise was echoing in a thousand different directions. Hashem militia is under attack again and they had to respond fast.

Hashem kept running with Angela towards the helicopter until they reached there. The paramedic helped Angela and the girl to climb in. Angela shouted at Hashem, "Hashem, get in."

Hashem did not look at her, he just ushered the pilot to fly away. The helicopter flew over the combatants, and Angela could see below Hashem and his troops entangled in a dreadful fight with Boko Haram militants. She saw Hashem and his troops standing like a rock stabbing Boko Haram militant in the heads, necks, chest and abdomens, spraying them with machine guns, and tearing them apart with grenades.

From the helicopter, the Boko Haram gunmen looked like chickens in a slaughterhouse yard, dead or fleeing in every direction.

CHAPTER 23

The helicopter landed in a military base. The girl was taken to an orphanage and Angela to Protea hotel. She had the feeling that Hashem will come to see her after the catastrophic events they witnessed together. Her trip to Nigeria was published in newspapers and announced in the media. Hashem must have known that she was going to visit the school she established in Gwoza village, and when the village was attacked, he had rushed forward to save her.

She kept thinking of Hashem. He was one of the richest men of the world, yet he was willing to sacrifice himself for a noble cause. He recruited armed force professionals and led them with great dash and fearlessness. His gallantry and devotion to his mission were conspicuous examples to his men. They followed him like fierce lions and performed deeds of valour.

She missed Hashem so much. She wanted to feel his warm chest against her and his protecting arms around her again. In hope of seeing him again, she stayed in the hotel for more days.

As night crept in, she heard a knock on the door. She opened it to see Hashem standing staring at her with eyes like kindling flames. Being frenzied with sexual lust after his relentless fights, his desire flared darkly in his eyes. It was the same look he would give her when he was going to take her in a violent way. She knew that in such condition of severe lust, he could have sex four times a day and never be happy with anything less than seven days a week.

The fierce battles with Boko Haram however, numbed her emotions and spoiled her sex drive. She needed time to recover and be normal again, but when she saw lust in Hashem eyes, she decided to give herself to him freely, enjoying the sense of belonging and protection in his arms.

Hashem grabbed her wrist and demanded, "Come to bed." Her mind went blank; her body went limp as she walked with him to the bedroom. He ripped her clothes off, and pushed her onto bed. He took off his clothes and mounted her in a rush. He kissed her roughly bruising her mouth. He had not shaved and the bristles burned her face. He was cruel in his love making, as if intending to punish her. He hovered over her, his eyes heavy lidded and predatory expression of sexual need on his face. He made love to her like a wild wolf. He made her crazier for him than ever. She enjoyed his brutal touches and his bruising mouth. She had never felt so filled before.

He made love to her again and again, taking her high and hard so that her climax crashed over her and left her shuddering and gasping against him.

When the passion subsided, she basked in his heat savouring the scent of him. She rested her head against his chest listening to the steady beat of his heart.

He had not uttered a word since she opened the door for him. She knew he was mad at her. She could see this in his eyes that looked as hard stones.

"You seem mad at me. I want to talk to you and yet you do not seem to want to talk. I am tired of being alone listening to the sound of my tears. So, let me do all the talking." She said kissing him tenderly on the lips then resting her head on his chest.

"I enjoyed being ravished, being lovingly—yet forcefully—taken by the man I love. I liked it because I felt beautiful and desired. It was some of the best sex we have ever had. I love to be wanted that way.

"It is useless to anguish over something, which has been done that we cannot change. Healthy people make amends, and move on with life.

"We fell in love, despite our differences, and once we did, something rare and beautiful was created. Love is sharing and forgiving. It is loyalty through good and bad times. I can't stop loving you. You blow me away. I never imagined loving someone the way that I love you. A man cannot live without love, and I am your love. Please do not go, I love you."

As if she remembered something important, she lifted her head up and looked into his eyes begging, "There is no greater torture in this life than for a mother to live without her son. I cannot stand the thought of never seeing Amr again. If I could wish one thing, I would hear him call me mom. Hashem, please, I want to see my son. I break down every time I think about it."

She continued: 'It's tough to raise a little girl without a mom'. Bring Aisha with Amr. Let's live together as one good family."

She felt his arms tightening around her as if reassuring her that her request will be fulfilled.

"Enough talking now. You have worn me out. I need some sleep." She stretched her body beside him and fell into a deep sleep.

When she woke up in the morning, she found herself alone in bed. Hashem's side was empty, and that told her that he was still angry with her. He used her body to satisfy his desire, and not because he missed her or loved her. She loved him deeply, but he seemed distant and not caring for her anymore. He disappeared without a word. She was scared he would forget about her and that she might lose him forever. Losing something so close to her, is like losing herself.

CHAPTER 24

Hashem was at his office reading some papers when his telephone buzzed. It was his secretary calling, "sorry Mr. Hashem for the interruption but Mrs Angela Collins will be a guest on the TV Late Show. The program is about to begin."

Hashem picked up the remote and turned on his widescreen TV. Angela sat there looking older than her age and more matured. A red slash of lipstick and her brown hair piled up. She was dressed in a silky dress that hugged her body the way he liked. Her long legs crossed showing her beautiful knees and legs. She looked pale but beautiful as always.

The interviewer came out of the backstage, sat down at his desk and introduced Angela to the audience.

"With the global economy in turmoil, women struggled to maintain their share of the Forbes list of the World's Billionaires. On the Forbes list, Mrs Angela Collins is one of the richest women in the United States." The interviewer said facing the camera.

The interviewer then turned his face to Angela and asked, "Mrs Angela, tell us about the essential elements of your success."

"I attribute my success to a tough upbringing by my father, who insisted that I always come in the top three in my class at school. He taught me that complaining solves absolutely nothing. He never uttered a negative thing about anyone or complaining about his work. More importantly, he made certain that I realize how fortunate I am to have what I had. My dad was a marketing genius. He was profoundly good at negotiating because he could turn negative concerns into positive attributes almost magically."

"You are known as a tough working woman; tell us about your achievements."

"I have always been a bit ambitious. I believe in hard work. I have no time for friends. I like to be a leader. I am an action oriented person. I am a big fan of just getting out in action mode, swinging at my goals and getting the instant gratification of seeing the results."

"But what do you need for goal achievement to succeed in the long-term?"

"One of the most important functions of leaders is to articulate the vision and create opportunities for team members to thrive. In doing so, leaders understand the organization's heartbeat and determine effective methods to influence employees to perform at optimum levels goal achievement."

"During the financial crisis, your company faced lack of funds and had to be merged with a company from the Gulf Estate!" The interviewer added.

"Yes, I had a merge with another company but I managed to buy the shares of my partner and purchase two other companies working in related fields."

"With all this success, are you happy Mrs Angela?"

"I am still recovering from the loss of my child, and the separation from my husband." She said after a silent sadness.

"Every human walk around with a certain kind of sadness. Do not let past relationships upset you. Fight the sadness and try to be happy."

"I want to be happy but something inside me screams that I do not deserve it."

"You are a wealthy woman, does money bring happiness?"

"Money can add to happiness, but does not directly cause it."

"What is your idea for happiness?"

"Happiness is the meaning and the purpose of life, the whole aim and end of human existence. Happiness is only real when shared. Happiness is holding someone in your arms and knowing you hold the whole world. I found happiness in the arms of the man I loved."

"We know that you are a brave woman. Your success in business proves that. What is the bravest thing you have ever done."

"Continuing my life when I wanted to die."

"You have passed through a lot of pain Mrs Angela. What is the worst kind of pain you faced?"

"When you are smiling just to stop the tears from falling."

"And what is the saddest thing you have seen?"

"To love someone who used to love you."

"Do you cry sometimes Mrs Angela?"

"My tears no longer flow; my eyes are tired of weeping."

"You do not mind if I ask you a personal question?"

"Not at all."

"We know that you broke up with your husband after a long marriage. Are you separated or divorced?"

"We are separated not divorced."

"You have been separated for so many years. Why not getting a divorce?"

"He thinks I am a part of his life that must remain intact and alive - I am the mother of his children."

"But he abandoned you in a most dire situation!"

"I don't blame him. He loved me crazily even though I had a million annoying habits that can drive him nuts. He loved me with all my boobs, but my boobs were bigger. He forgave all my flaws and mistakes until he couldn't take it any longer."

"Do you still love him after this long separation?"

"He rescued me from ruin. He charmed my heart with unconditional love. He is the only man who would make me feel special and beautiful. He is my only love. He is my man, my hero. There is no other man who could ever take his place."

"Your loyalty to him after what he did to you is really admirable. In just few words, what are you exactly to him?"

"I am a special fragrance he likes to inhale." She said after a long pause.

"Do you have anything to say to him through this program?"

She faced the camera with tearful eyes and said without hesitation, "You are the only man I have ever loved, the only man I have ever wanted. You broke my heart and left me chattered. Please come and gather the broken pieces, heal my soul and make me smile again." The words died away in her throat. The sadness in the tone of her words spoke volumes.

In spite of her arrogance, she had humility enough to confess her errors and to retrace her steps back. Hashem's heart melted at her words. It took him a moment to realize that his eyes were filled with tears.

CHAPTER 25

There was a portrait of a lady painted in 1840 Angela wanted to acquire. The picture was for sale in Brunk Auctions - Asheville, NC. The auction will sell the picture to the highest bidder. The participants bid openly against one another, with each subsequent bid required to be higher than the previous bid.

It was an ascending bid auction. Bidders continued to increase the price until there were only two bidders left, Angela and a man who was persistently raising the bid to above the reasonable price. He kept bidding up the picture to reach a higher level. If Angela kept bidding against him, she was going to pay three or four times more than she should have. The auction started with a bid of one million dollars and reached 10 million dollars. This was insane, Angela thought, but in many auctions, the most irrational person wins. The auctioneer raised the price to eleven million dollars, and the man raised his hand accepting the new price. Angela however declined, feeling sorry for her terrible loss.

The auctioneer announced: "The picture was sold to Mrs Angela Collins – the price is eleven million dollars."

Angela was extremely amazed, she stared at the other bidder who left his seat and approached her. "I am a proxy calling out bids on Mr. Hashem's behalf. This is your birthday present Mrs Collins." The man said smiling.

Tears came rushing into her eyes: "Where is Mr. Hashem now?" She exclaimed.

"Right now he is in London."

A yearning ached through her with such power that she felt life without him was a nightmare. She whispered in her heart: "I miss you so much it hurts. I will love you until I die, and if there is life after that, I will love you then."

Through the glass panorama windows of her office, Angela stood gazing out at the city. The awareness of being "above it all" elated her. Now she is on top of the world. Forbes magazine evaluated her as one amongst the top 50 influential women in the world today. Arms crossed, and hugging herself, she kept looking at the views of the city. The city looked bright and fresh, its building aglow, the skyscrapers sparkling in the sunlight.

She whispered to herself behind her heart: "I am a very independent woman and does not need you anymore. I hate you for the way you treated me. I would never forget how you hit me, humiliated me, ignored me and abandoned me during times of distress. You deprived me from my only son and fed him hatred against his own mama. You do not deserve my interest or care. I no longer love you. I can live without you. I will not succumb to your charm. You are a past phase of my life, that was gone dead and buried. I will not bow, I will not break, and without you, I can shove the world away. No man is worth my tears. Sigh no more, Angela, sigh no more."

Suddenly tears welled in her eyes. She whispered in agony, "O God please help me. I am not just falling apart, I am broken. He is the only person I can ever imagine myself with. I want him back."

Angela stepped back to return to her desk but she saw her son Amr and his sister Aisha, and Hashem standing by the door. All the elation and rejection she felt moments ago had subsided and turned into a tremendous yearning.

She stretched her arms out to Amr and Aisha as she knelt to the ground. They ran to her and she gathered them up in her arms. She cried and laughed raining their faces with her kisses. Her cries grew worse but she kept rocking them and holding them tightly as if afraid, they would disappear.

The secretary came in. "Where is Hashem? He was standing here at the door?" Angela asked the secretary through her tears.

"He just left few moments ago."

"Take my son and his sister home and make sure they are comfortable and happy."

She ran out of the door and down the stairs to the street. She saw Hashem walking down the pavement heading towards his car. She called his name, he turned back to see her gasping for air and abundant tears streaming down her face. She walked up to him and began trembling from head to toe. She grasped tightly to the front of his shirt and tugged him down toward her.

"What do you want woman?" He said harshly.

"Take me to your place and make love to me…please." Her words tumbled out hurriedly, her face reddening with embarrassment. Her chest heaving as she struggled to control her breathing.

"This is really upsetting. How dare you ask me to sleep with you as if nothing happened between us! Haven't you any decency left?"

He knew that her desire was not only for lust, but also to be encapsulated in his protected arms and feel safe again.

"I am still your wife, am I not? There is no shame in being hungry for you. There is no shame in longing to share my life with you. I love you so hard, and even with my flaws, I am worth living don't you think?" Tears streaming down her face as she tried to smile.

His strong love rose up, battled with him and conquered.

"Come." He said grabbing her hand and walking her to the car. He opened the car door for her and she climbed into the front passenger seat. The car roared to his fancy apartment.

In the bedroom, they stripped off quickly and threw their clothes on the floor. He pushed her roughly onto the bed and rolled over upon her. She clung to him hungry for his reassurance and protection. She wrapped her arms around him welcoming him. She kissed him with her own hunger; her lips devoured his as her tongue fought to consume his. Hashem loved Angela's body. It was still beautiful after having two children and seemed to be even more voluptuous than ever. He kissed her with all the longing, all the love he felt for her.

"I missed you so much." She whispered as she breathed into his mouth. His lovemaking was strong and harsh. He thrust so deep and so hard that she gagged from the violent motion. Her pleasured scream oozed out of her mouth as her body shuddered uncontrollably. He wanted to torment her, to subdue her. This time it was not only lust, he was asserting his authority over her. By subduing her, he would preserve his own power and dignity.

He took pleasure in inflicting pain; he teased, tormented and tortured her, putting her through a sensual hell. When he felt that she was about to explode, he took her wildly as if she were mare daring to be tamed. He brought her to orgasm repeatedly, and each time her body exploded with ultimate pleasure. The torment became more intense, more frenzied than the last, and each orgasm hit her with the shattering power of an earthquake, but the pain he sought to inflict was pleasure to her.

"God, you made me feel so good, so alive." She said enjoying the delicious feeling of being in his arms. A deep sense of security washed over her. She whispered against his lips I missed you so much, don't ever leave me again."

"After what you did to me, I think I am numb from the neck down." She said spent from the fierce of his lovemaking.

"Hashem, let's forget what happened in the past, it is the future that counts." She said and sunk from weariness into a deep sleep.

It was a beautiful bright morning, the sun lit up the room. Turning to her side, she watched his sleeping figure. Dear God she had missed him so much, he was with her now and that was all that mattered.

Hashem woke up in the morning to see Angela sitting beside him in bed.

"Good morning darling. Did you sleep well?" she said smiling.

"Yes, you have worn me out, woman". She bent down and kissed his lips.

"I will make you breakfast." He said raising himself up in the bed.

"No darling, you stay here, I will make you breakfast. She raised her hand signalling him to stay.

"I am afraid if you leave the bed; you may go somewhere and disappear for another seven years." She said while leaving the bed and wrapping her naked body in his white robe.

"What do you want for breakfast dear?"

"Scrambled eggs and bread and butter."

"I will have the same." She said disappearing in the kitchen.

Angela returned with a large breakfast tray. She laid it across the bed. They were both famished. They ate with good appetite. After they finished eating, Angela took the tray away from the bed and placed it on the bedside table. She then sat in bed on her knees staring onto him for a long moment.

A sudden wave of sadness overtook her. Suddenly she slammed her hands hard against his chest in reprimand.

"Fucking idiot. How dare you walk out on me like that? You treated me with unrelenting cruelty. I feel inadequate, cheated, betrayed, and tormented. I have waited and waited and waited, but you did not even care to open the door and walk through to find the woman who was waiting to receive your love. The love you gave me yesterday - the love that revived my soul and eased my pain. You do not know what it was like. It was torture being away from you. You tortured me by not making love to me all these years. Can you give me the last seven years of my life back?" She burst into tears unable to restrain herself.

Her weeping only angered him. He shot her an angry look," you hurt me, you humiliated me. What is the matter with you –you want me to bring that up now?"

Despite his angered glare still painted onto his face, she could see the tears in his eyes. She threw herself in his arms and cried her heart out. He held her tight and wept bitter tears with her.

"My heart has been bleeding since the day I hurt you. Please forgive me." She said sobbing.

He felt her agony. He soothed her with comforting words, rocking her in his arms, "Hush. Stop crying," but she couldn't stop weeping.

He stroked her back, pressing gentle kisses at the top of her hair. Slowly she lifted her gaze to his, tears slipping down her cheeks.

"I am nothing without you. Having you in my life is all that matters. Why can't you see who I truly am? I love you. Please forgive me."

"You are forgiven. Now put yourself back together again."

You won't leave me, will you Hashem? She said staring at him with frightened eyes.

"I am not sure about that. I cannot stand the pain of living with you anymore. We have to talk."

Her heart sank into the pit of her stomach. Her heartbeat began to speed up. He saw her eyes filled with so much pain.

"Okay! I won't leave you, but on one condition – you behave."

"Yes, my love, whatever you say."

"Let's make a deal."

"Say what you need to say. I will be your humble and obedient servant."

I hate foul-mouthed women. I do not want you to utter one foul word in my presence – you hear me?"

"Yes, my love I hear you."

"You humiliate me in public with your foul words, this is emotional abuse. Do you understand?"

"Yes, my love I understand."

"Hold your tongue Angela. You have just called me, 'fucking idiot!' You are going to have to learn to hold your tongue instead of saying whatever comes into your head. Stop being rude and behave respectfully. You need to mind your manners and get control of yourself."

"Yes sir. I will be the politest woman you have ever known." She said kissing his lips and cheeks.

"Stop being jealous - your jealousy humiliates me before the people."

"I am sorry for being jealous. It is just that I am afraid of losing the best thing to have ever happened to me. I will not be jealous, I give you my word."

"I don't want you to get angry. It does not make me feel good. Feeling passionate about something doesn't mean you have to be angry. You are a danger to yourself when you get angry."

"Sometimes, you have to get angry to get things done. If we were to lose the ability to be angry, to be outraged, we would be robots. And I refuse that."

"Do not give me this crap Angela. When you are angry, you degenerate into a crockery throwing, foul-mouthed. Getting angry does not solve anything." He said angrily.

"Feeling angry is a human phenomenon. The capacity to feel angry and to respond in some way to that feeling is in us from birth. It is as basic as feeling hungry, tired, lonely, loving, or…

He cut her off, "God damn it! You steal a man's arguments as if that proves anything!"

"See how you are angry? Please do not be angry darling because anger is bad for your health." She said laughing mockingly.

"Promise me to control your anger. You must not ever let your anger take control of you. Do not let yourself lose control, okay? Promise me that."

"I promise, love." She said kissing his neck and bare chest.

"The day is young and we have nothing to do. What to do now?" He said leaving the bed.

Let's wander through the city with your hand in mine. Let's take

a casual walk around the block? Let's mingle with pedestrians and enjoy fresh air." She suggested.

She put her clothes on, and he changed into casual jeans and T-shirt, and off to hustle and bustle of the street. They walked on the pavement laughing. Angela spotted a stunning woman coming their way. The woman was smiling seductively at Hashem. The way the woman looked at him, the way her eyes swallowed his whole as if he already belonged to her, caused a feeling of nausea within Angela. A wave of jealousy washed over her. Her left hand began to shake convulsively. She leaned heavily against Hashem and grabbed his right arm to stop the shaking.

"Hey, you dislocate my shoulder. Stop leaning heavily on me I am not going anywhere!" He said amazed at her sudden movement.

When the woman passed them, she stopped after a few meters looking back at Hashem with a seductive smile. Angela turned around to see the woman standing still smiling.

Angela exploded in jealous anger and stormed at her: "What are you looking at bitch?"

Hashem yelled at Angela, "Haven't we agreed that you behave yourself?" A frown crept across his face.

"Darling haven't you seen how she was staring at you. This woman is a slut."

He shot her an angry look. His angry expression then faded and slowly a smile stretched his lips. His smile got bigger and bigger and turned into a big laugh. He laughed until tears came into his eyes.

"O God, you make me feel good. I love you." Angela squealed like a child and jumped into his arms kissing him all over his face.

www.ingramcontent.com/pod-product-compliance
Ingram Content Group UK Ltd.
Pitfield, Milton Keynes, MK11 3LW, UK
UKHW041828200726
13854UKWH00002BA/882